# The First Year

# The First Year

By Crystal Liechty

Bonneville Books
Springville, Utah

No part of this book may be reproduced in any form whatsoever, whether by graphic, visual, electronic, film, microfilm, tape recording, or any other means, without prior written permission of the publisher, except in the case of brief passages embodied in critical reviews and articles.

ISBN 13: 978-1-55517-982-7
ISBN 10: 1-55517-982-7

Published by Bonneville Books, an imprint of
Cedar Fort, Inc., 2373 W. 700 S., Springville, UT, 84663
Distributed by Cedar Fort, Inc., www.cedarfort.com

LIBRARY OF CONGRESS CATALOGING-IN-PUBLICATION DATA

Liechty, Crystal.
  The First year / by Crystal Liechty.
    p. cm.
  ISBN 1-55517-982-7 (acid-free paper)
  1. Married people--Fiction. 2.  Marital conflict--Fiction. 3.  Mormons--Fiction. I.
  Title.

PS3612.I3353F57 2006
813'.6--dc22

                                                      2006027349

Cover design by Nicole Williams
Cover design © 2006 by Lyle Mortimer
Printed in the United States of America

10  9  8  7  6  5  4  3  2  1

Printed on acid-free paper

# Dedication

To Jessica Penrose and Scott Liechty.

# Acknowledgments

SPECIAL THANKS TO Sallie Mattison Young, James Dashner, Josi Kilpack, Tiffany Pyper, Emily Young, Lily Webb, and the Wright family.

# Chapter 1 ———————

"WHAT EVER HAPPENED TO taffeta?" I sighed, following my best friend, Angel, into the ladies' room.

"What?"

"Taffeta. No one wears taffeta anymore." I glanced around the bathroom. "JoJo? Are ya in here?"

It was the end of January, and JoJo, a friend from high school, was about to tie the knot. If I could find her.

"Do you know what taffeta *is*?" Angel asked.

I thought for a moment. "Not really. But I like the word. Taffeta. Taffeta, taffeta, taffeta."

"You might be legally insane," Angel said.

"Name-calling, again." I tsk-tsked, swirling around and admiring my reflection in the mirror. "I feel like a princess."

Angel snorted and examined her own reflection. We stood side by side in matching pale pink satin dresses with bell sleeves and full skirts. My blonde hair was pulled up into my interpretation of a fancy bun, while Angel wore her dark hair loose with full curls falling just below her shoulders. I hated her perfect hair. I wanted to blow my nose in it.

"While I agree that we're absolutely breathtaking," Angel said, "I believe we've lost sight of our mission. We still have no JoJo."

"Seriously, though." I scrunched my nose at my reflection. "What's with the harsh lighting in bathrooms? I prefer a softer bulb, but you do pull off 'fluorescent' surprisingly well."

It's funny how people are never happy with what they have, because where I was thin and graceful, Angel was curvy and seductive, and we always complained of wishing to look more like the other.

"Why, thank you." Angel puckered her lips and struck a pose, admiring her reflection.

"Hey, movie star," I said, snapping my fingers in front of Angel's nose.

She frowned at me, and I pointed past my reflection toward a closed stall behind it, where white silk spilled underneath the door.

"Ah." she nodded.

Before we could devise a tactful way to wrench JoJo from her hideout, someone burst into the bathroom amidst a cloud of Eau de White Lily perfume.

"How's the bride?" asked an older woman whose name I'd forgotten moments after hearing it.

"I think she's trying not to throw up." I nodded toward the bathroom stall.

The woman rushed over and tapped gently on the metal door. "JoJo? Honey? Are you okay?"

"I'm wust fweeling a wiffle wijjy," JoJo mumbled.

"Uh . . ." the woman glanced at Angel and me for help, but we just shrugged. "Do you want me to get your mom, JoJo?"

"En a minufe I'll fe fine."

"Uh, okay, then." The woman tossed us a worried smile and hurried out of the bathroom.

"Seriously, JoJo." I leaned against the stall door that separated us. "Every bride gets a case of nerves before her big day, but you're starting to worry us."

"Um-hmm."

"So . . . what are you doing in there?" I waited for an answer but only heard muffled sniffling.

I glanced at Angel, who watched me through the mirror. She spun around and gestured to the stall beside the one JoJo was in. I nodded.

"I'm wust fweeling a wiffle wijjy," JoJo insisted.

Angel and I crept into the stall beside her and jumped onto the toilet seat, peeking over the edge. JoJo glanced up at us in surprise, her mouth full of toilet paper, her eyes full of tears.

"Oh, honey," Angel gushed. "Why are you crying? Is it really that bad?"

"What do you mean?" I scoffed at Angel. "You cried like a baby on your wedding day."

"No," Angel corrected. "I cried after I met Danny's *mom*. I was fine on my wedding day."

"Oh, right." I nodded and then turned back to JoJo. "So is your mother-in-law that bad?"

JoJo snorted and pulled the toilet paper out of her mouth, grimacing and picking stray pieces of toilet paper off her tongue.

Squeezing the ball of toilet paper in her hands, she sighed. "It's not that. It's not her . . . I'm just nervous, I guess."

"Are you sure you're ready to go through with this?" I tried not to stare at the crooked mascara lines under her eyes. "Are you sure you know Ted well enough yet?"

"You think I can call off my wedding an *hour* before it starts?" JoJo scoffed, blowing her nose in the ball of toilet paper.

"Well, has a dowry been exchanged, yet?" I asked.

Angel laughed. "Were you an eight-cow wife?"

"You guys are really helpful, you know that?" JoJo sniffled.

"C'mon, JoJo Mojo," I prodded. "Look at you. You're a mess. You can't get married in your condition."

"Yes," Angel agreed. "You're in no condition."

"But I—"

"What can we do, doctor?" I asked, turning to Angel.

We exchanged mischievous smiles, both of us determined not to let the concern we felt for JoJo show on our faces.

"There's only one possible cure but it's very risky. Very experimental."

"What is it, doctor? We'll do anything." Though I had no idea where Angel was going with this joke, I knew whatever suggestion she made would be better than forcing a moment of honest sincerity with JoJo.

"Road trip to Vegas."

"Road trip!" I exclaimed, jumping up, causing Angel to lose her balance, her left foot landing in the toilet bowl with a thunk.

"Beth!"

"Oops." I helped her back onto the seat. "Sorry."

"Yeah, I'm really going to take advice from you guys," JoJo said, rolling her eyes. She swished out of the stall and stopped in front of the mirror, patting her hair into place and wiping the mascara streaks off her face.

Angel and I walked up and stood on either side of her, waiting in silence.

"So, does this mean no road trip?" I finally asked.

"Do you have any idea how much this reception hall cost?" JoJo exclaimed.

"Nope." I shook my head. "I got married in the Salt Lake Temple. That was free."

"I got married in my parents' backyard," Angel said. "Also free."

"Well, then, don't talk to me about road trips," JoJo snapped.

The force of her response made me take a step back.

"And here I was, worried you were going through with this for the wrong reasons," I muttered to myself.

JoJo was the tallest of us, at five feet nine inches, with long strawberry blonde hair and a face that looked porcelain and perfectly formed—which hid an underlying sense of worthlessness that only showed itself in late-night confessions, her old poetry, and her choice in men.

"Can you just go get my mom?" JoJo asked. "She's got some aspirin in her purse."

"Sure, Mojo Toe Jam," I said. "You sure you're gonna be all right?"

JoJo nodded and gave me a reassuring smile.

"What do you think is really wrong with her?" Angel asked when we were down the hall and well out of earshot.

"She looks like she's barely holding it together, doesn't she?"

"Yeah." Angel thought for a moment. "I know I had a hard time with Danny and all, but that was mostly dealing with his family. I mean, the getting married part was the only thing that felt right to me."

"I know what you mean." I nodded. "The planning, the meeting the family, the trying not to flirt with strange men anymore—it all sucks. But the getting-married part is generally good stuff."

We stopped in front of a set of large wooden doors. I could hear chatter on the other side, mingled with the smell of roses and chocolate.

"How long has she been dating—uh—what was his name again?" Angel rested her shoulder against the door frame, cocking one foot over the other.

"Ted," I answered. "I think it's been about two months. Her boss set them up."

I glanced at two small girls who accidently rammed into each other as they ran by, causing them both to fall to the ground and erupt into giggles.

"The one from the mortgage company?" When I nodded, she shuddered. "Wasn't he a little psycho?"

"No," I said, turning back to Angel. "He was a lot psycho. He was obsessed with JoJo, but she wasn't having it. I think he set her up with his friend as a way to trick her into hanging out with *him* outside of work."

"That's a great way to start a marriage."

"Omigosh! Beth? Angel?" a shrill voice screamed. "Is that you guys? Omigosh. How *are* you?"

We both turned to see Chandra Higgs, who was leaning through a doorway down the hall from us.

"Chandra, how are you?" I feigned enthusiasm. Angel nodded and hid her grimace under a smile.

A former classmate, Chandra was the girl in high school who thought she was friends with everyone, brushing off the many ignored phone calls and forgotten party invites as small misunderstandings.

"I asked you first." She stepped into the hallway and walked up to us, grabbing my hands and shaking them. Hard.

"I'm good. Great." I struggled for something to say. "I'm married now."

"I heard." She dropped my hands and folded her arms, adopting an exaggerated pout.

"Yup. I'm Mrs. Loxstedt now. Kinda makes me feel old."

"And why wasn't I invited?"

"We eloped," I lied. "What with me being eight months pregnant and all."

Angel let out a loud snort and pretended to be intensely interested in the wall to her left.

"You?" Chandra laughed and shook her finger at me. "Nice try. I know you got married in the temple. Everyone was talking about it. We were all so surprised."

As if her incessant flirting with any member of the male gender wasn't bad enough, she had an ingenious way of disguising insults as compliments. Add to this a helping of incessant self-analysis inspired by *Dawson's Creek*, and the recipe for Chandra's personality is complete.

"Thanks. I think."

"But what about JoJo?" Chandra whispered, leaning toward me and gesturing around us. "I mean, this is a nice reception hall, but we all thought . . . well, you know."

In our world, there are only two ways to get married: in the temple and not in the temple. JoJo was fulfilling her destiny with the latter option and, as of yet, had not told me why.

"I know," I muttered, taking a step back.

While there are a lot of stipulations before someone is considered worthy to enter the temple (no smoking or drinking, pay tithing, be an active member of the Church), there's really only one requirement that keeps knocking people out of the running: Chastity.

"And you, little Miss Barlow . . . or should I say, Mrs. Snow." Chandra turned on Angel. "I hear the marriage bug bit you too."

"Yeah, but she went to the doctor and he assured her it's not infected," I said.

"Always making jokes." Chandra shook her head, smiling. "Always making everyone laugh."

"So how about you, Chandra?" Angel jumped in before I could respond. "You taken the plunge yet?"

"No." Chandra patted her hair. "I'm keeping my options open, but I'm currently accepting applications. Unfortunately, I've already had a look around, and your husbands are the cutest guys here. How long have y'all been married, now?"

"It's what? Two and a half months for Beth." Angel glanced at me and I nodded. "And just over a month for me."

"Oh, good, you still qualify for an annulment." Chandra slapped my shoulder and let out a shrill giggle. "I'm just kidding, of course. I'm sure y'all will be married for a very long time. I'm starting to feel old, though. Pretty soon I'll be the only single girl left from our grade."

"You should move out of Utah, then," I suggested, perhaps a little too eagerly. "Out there you're a freak if you're married before twenty-five, not after."

"Good point," Chandra agreed, completely missing the intention of my remark. "We're only twenty-one, aren't we?"

"I'm actually twenty-two," Angel said.

"And I'm really only fourteen."

Chandra laughed. "You *look* like you're only fourteen."

I opened my mouth and then clamped it shut, glancing at Angel, who was hiding a smile.

"Well, I'll come find y'all later," Chandra said. "I'm gonna see if I can get a peek at the groom. After all, he's not the groom yet."

"She's evil," I muttered as Angel and I watched her saunter off.

"The root of."

"Do I really look like I'm only fourteen?"

"C'mon, Beth." Angel opened the door to the main dining room. "We've got a wedding to save."

# Chapter 2

*An ideal marriage is a true partnership between two imperfect people, each striving to complement the other, to keep the commandments, and to do the will of the Lord.*

—Russell M. Nelson, "Our Sacred Duty to Honor Women," *Ensign,* May 1999, 39

Six months later

*"There has been a lot of debate over the centuries as to what really took place that day in the Garden of Eden." My eyes dart around the dark office, landing everywhere but on Dr. Farb. "Is the apple a symbol? Did the serpent exist? Was it really all the woman's fault? No one can say for sure what really happened."*

*This is my third therapy session with him, and every time I come, it gets harder to look him in the eye.*

*"But I know the truth," I say, nodding to myself. "Adam left the toilet seat up again for the millionth time, and Eve decided it was payback time. Eternal-damnation style."*

*I find myself rambling like a nervous teenager in answer to every question he asks. It gets so bad at times that I've formed the habit of stopping midsentence, sucking in a deep breath, and clamping my mouth shut until the ensuing silence is interrupted by another question from Dr. Farb. At which point the process begins again.*

"That's a unique theory, Beth. Why do you feel that way?" Dr. Farb leans back in his seat and clicks open his pen, taking my vehemence in stride.

"Okay, maybe I'm being a little dramatic, but if the very first couple—who even hung out with God on occasion—couldn't get it right, where's the hope for the rest of us?"

"You don't feel like there's hope for you?"

"I don't know. Should I? It's barely our first year of marriage and I'm already in therapy because of him."

I blink hard, annoyed at Dr. Farb for causing a lump to form in my throat. He's so superior and . . . and calm all the time. It's absolutely maddening.

"What about your friends?" Dr. Farb asks, running the pen down the side of his notebook and pausing. "You've mentioned your friend JoJo's wedding a few times. What was the significance of that event for you?"

"JoJo's wedding was a mess. It was like a Monet. Far away, everything looked shiny and perfect, but up close, we had a panic-stricken bride, two food-related injuries, and at least three catfights—only one of which I was directly involved in."

I smirk at the memory; Dr. Farb's expression doesn't change.

"So, if she were here, what would you like to say to her?"

"It's not just her. I've been to a lot of weddings over the past year, and I've got a whole list of basics that I think every bride should follow."

I grow more animated, encouraging the change in topic. I'm in no danger of tearing up at the memory of JoJo's wedding.

"First of all, don't invite your ex-boyfriends. I know the urge to show them what a great loss they've suffered by letting you go is very strong, but it adds unnecessary drama to an already dramatic event." I slap one hand into the other as I make each point. "If you must rub in the nuptials, then have a mutual friend casually show them your engagement photo and act surprised and embarrassed when the ex mentions that he did not receive an invitation.

"And if you're going to make your bridesmaids pay for their own dresses, then you don't get to pick them out. Fair enough? Okay, moving on."

*Dr. Farb watches me, waiting for me to say more.*

I continue: "I know there is a general consensus that your wedding day is supposed to be the most important day of your life and that loved ones should spoil you and all that, but this does not give you leave to be a shrieking harpy.

"I'm sorry the flowers on your cake are purple and not violet and the ring bearer burped while making his way down the aisle, but locking yourself in the bathroom and screaming through the door is not going to make the day go any better."

*Dr. Farb opens his mouth to speak, but I mow him over, determined to make it through the remainder of the session without talking about anything that really matters to me.*

"And obviously, this should go without saying, but make sure you actually want to marry the person you're going to marry." *I lean back in the chair, throwing my leg over the armrest.* "I know how it can be if you're a single Mormon girl. You're watching all your friends take the plunge, giggling and making annoying innuendoes that they're sure you wouldn't understand, while your Mom is dropping obvious hints about some new returned missionary who just got a scholarship to BYU.

"But I would say it's far worse to be the one who gets a divorce after only six months of marriage and shortly thereafter descends into a constant state of debauchery—shaking a fist at the temple and throwing empty cans of Red Bull at passing missionaries."

"It seems like you've spent some time thinking about this," *he observes.* "Why is that?"

"Okay, maybe I'm exaggerating, but I'm still a little miffed that JoJo married a guy that I hadn't even met until the wedding day."

"Why does that upset you?" *Dr. Farb asks, scribbling something on his notepad.*

"Because."

*Dr. Farb remains silent.*

"Because we're friends. Since high school. It's bad enough that she's marrying him after two months. How does she know this guy isn't a total creep?"

"And if he was? What do you think you could have done about it?" Dr. Farb asks.

"Warn her, at least. Sabotage the wedding, at best."

"Do you feel responsible for how your friends' lives are going?"

"No. I mean, I don't know. Maybe. I want to help them. Sometimes you can't see things as clearly in your own life, so it's good to have friends you can trust that can . . . you know, point stuff out to you."

"Do you listen to your friends' advice regarding your life?" Dr. Farb flips to a new page in his notebook and makes a note.

"How could I? With the mess they're all making of their lives? Maybe it sounds harsh, but every day I've got someone calling me in some sort of desperate situation that they can't handle on their own. I've got my hands full between Angel and Lady alone."

Dr. Farb flips back a few pages. "Angel is your best friend and Lady's your older sister, correct? Do they know how you feel about the way they are leading their lives?"

"What do you mean?"

"I'm hearing a lot of resentment about how much they depend on you," Dr. Farb says. "It sounds like you're saying that the people in your life need you so much that you don't feel like you can lean on them at all. Is that correct?"

I swallow, frowning at Dr. Farb and pulling my knees up to my chin.

"Well, I didn't mean it like that. I mean, I've never even thought of it like that before. I guess I like being the one who's needed. The one who has it together and is in control."

"Do you believe you are in control of your life right now?" Dr. Farb asks.

"That's a silly question." I snort, glancing at the clock. "Why would I be here if I was?"

# Chapter 3

"BETH, I'M SO GLAD you answered!" Angel's voice screeched through my cell phone.

I held the phone away from my ear and grimaced. "Calm down, Angel. Deep breaths."

There was a pause as Angel collected herself.

"So?" I asked a moment later.

"I just got back from Danny's parents' house—"

"Ah. 'Nuff said."

"No. You won't believe what she said to me this time."

I fell back on my couch and propped my feet up on the coffee table, phone pressed against my ear. Might as well get comfortable. I nodded for her to proceed. As if she could see me, she launched into her diatribe.

"So, we're all sitting there talking and stuff. And everyone starts sharing kid stories and experiences from Primary. And I

don't know how, but this leads to Danny's mom and sister singing some random Primary song . . ."

I'd been peppering "uh-huhs" throughout this speech.

"And Danny's mom stops in the middle of the song and asks
me why I'm not singing—in front of everybody. I mean, everybody was there—Danny's dad, brother, sister, his sister's boyfriend, their friend, and his girlfriend. And so everyone is just
staring at me, you know? And what does Danny do? Nothing. So
I say, 'I don't remember all the words,' and Danny's mom gasps.
She *gasps,* Beth."

I gasped.

"And she says all worried-like, 'You don't remember the
words? Did you ever know them?' And what does Danny do?
Nothing. I mean, I'm twenty-two years old, and she's all huffy
because I don't remember the words to a song that I haven't sung
in, what? Thirteen years?"

"What did you do?"

"I dunno. I just sat there like an idiot. I mean, she looked so
sad, Beth. Sad. Are adults really like this?"

"From what I've seen, it—" I stopped at the sound of my
doorbell. "Oh, hold on a sec, Angel. I think someone's here."

I trudged across my apartment and peered through the peephole. There stood my older sister, leaning into the door. Her face
looked like a large, round balloon with her body as the tiny string
fading beneath her.

"Beth, open up," she called through the door. "Please."

This last word was more of a whimper, followed by a thud, as
her head fell against the door.

"Angel, I'm gonna have to call you back. Lady's here. Okay
. . . I know . . . okay . . . talk to you later . . . bye . . . okay . . .
bye."

I swung open the door and ushered Lady in. She was trying
valiantly not to pout.

"So, what's up?" I asked. "Are you okay?"

"Sure." She walked past me into my living room. I followed
her and stopped in the entryway, leaning against the wall.

Lady and I were opposites in every possible way. Her personality was open and friendly, eager to please, while I was stubborn and often sarcastic but fiercely loyal.

"Really?" I asked as she fell back onto my couch and stared up at me. "'Cause you kinda look like you just dropped your ice cream cone or something."

She made a face and stood. "Speaking of, got anything to drink? My mouth is sticky like marshmallows."

I followed her into the kitchen.

"Help yourself," I said. "What's mine is yours and all that."

"Do you have any Gatorade?" she asked, pushing aside a carton of milk.

I glanced at the last bottle of Gatorade in the door of the fridge and shook my head. "No, uh, I think we're all out. Sorry. Want a Coke? Water?"

"Never mind." She closed the refrigerator and turned to me, her eyes growing big and round. "I actually need to talk to you about something."

I nodded and led her back into the living room, where we sat across from each other in silence for a moment. This was a habit of ours. The more serious the problem, the longer the silence that preceded it. This was a long silence.

"Sheesh, Lady, what is it?" I exploded.

"I'm moving in with Chance," she squeaked.

I nodded. That explained it.

"Betsy? Betsy Boo?"

I shot her a dark look. I've asked her very nicely on several occasions to stop calling me that. It ranks right up there with the "wet willy" she still thinks is so funny to give me.

"Beth? Please say something."

"Well, what do you want me to say?" I snapped. "You know how I'm going to react. I think it's wrong. That's not going to stop you, is it? Are you trying to get my permission or something?"

"Chance says that since so many marriages end in divorce these days, it's a lot smarter to try living together first." Lady tugged at the hem of her shirt. "He says he really wants to marry me, but he made a pact with himself that he would live with the girl he married for two years before he did it. To make sure, you know?"

"That's the biggest pile of monkey droppings I've ever heard."

"Why?" Lady was defensive. "Just because it's not the way you think? You know I'm not active in the Church anymore. It's not like I'm going to have to go confess to my bishop or anything."

I looked at her sideways and made a farting sound with my mouth.

"I really love him." Her tone was bordering on superior.

I stared at her for a moment, searching for the right words.

"Lady, this isn't about the Church," I said. "It's about you. I don't want to see you get taken advantage of. It's fine if he wants to *date* you for two years, but live with you? It's like he's saying, 'I'm going to pretend to marry you because I'm too much of a coward to do it for real.' You deserve better than that."

"Sheesh, Beth." She looked at me in disgust. "You need to get out of Utah. In the real world, everybody lives together first. You're still in *Full House* and *Family Matters* mode and that's great for you, but the rest of us are over here with the *Friends* and *Sex and the City* reruns."

"First of all, nice pop culture reference," I said, holding up a finger. "And secondly, how is that a good reason? Like the rest of the world looks so happy right now? Did you ever consider that divorce is so high because people think that those TV shows are how their lives are supposed to look?"

"Excuse me, Dr. Phil," she said, "but do you really think Chance would want to marry me if I didn't let him move in first? He'd think I was hiding something or something."

I shook my head. "And I assume you're not planning to tell Mom?"

She let out a sharp laugh. "Yeah, right on that one."

"Well, thanks, Lady," I muttered. "Now I'm an accessory. Why did you even tell me?"

"Because I'm happy," she said. "And I'm scared, and I want you to be there for me. No matter what, right?"

"Yeah, yeah," I replied, shaking my head. "Hey, does JoJo still live in your apartment complex?"

"I don't know. Probably."

"I've been trying to get ahold of her forever. I've left, like, three messages and two e-mails. I haven't talked to her since her wedding."

"She's a newlywed; give her some space."

"I'm a newlywed. You don't see me falling off the face of the earth."

Lady sighed and stretched out her feet, pointing her toes and yawning. "La la la. Glad we got all that settled. Want to watch *Run Lola Run*? I'm going to teach myself Russian by osmosis."

"I thought it was in German," I said.

"Huh." Lady frowned and looked away, considering.

"Anyway, I've got to work tonight. In fact, I better get going," I said, glancing at my watch. "Maybe tomorrow."

"Okay." Lady picked up her bag and turned to me. "Promise you won't tell Mom?"

I nodded.

"Promise you'll come visit us after we get settled?"

I nodded.

"Promise you'll let me borrow your *Pirates of the Caribbean* DVD?"

I pushed her out the door.

When I got home from work at Barnes and Noble that night, I was in a sour mood.

I threw off my coat and fell onto the couch next to Mike, who was staring at the television. I glanced at the screen. Basketball. Big shocker, there.

Mike had played every sport in high school, but basketball is by far his favorite.

I put my chin on his shoulder and stared up at him coyly. With his boyish good looks and easygoing manner, Mike could reduce a pro wrestler on steroids to giggles, but the thing I loved most about him was how he never quite understood why people liked him so much. He honestly believed he was a big nerd and that the people who clamored for his approval simply hadn't noticed yet.

"Mike?" I made my voice sound soft and seductive.

He ignored me.

I batted my eyelashes.

He ignored me.

I wiggled a little closer.

He ignored me.

I let out a heavy sigh and leaned the other way.

He glanced at me and smiled absently.

"How was work, honey?"

"Oh, now I'm in the room," I muttered.

"What?"

"I've been home forever and you're just now acknowledging my presence."

I could feel the itch coming on. The itch for a fight. I am a great master of this, though I would never admit it aloud. It doesn't matter what he says next. I will twist his words and throw them back at him.

I will continue to do this until he gets frustrated and yells at me. Then I will storm into the bedroom and slam the door. This is followed by an hour of pouting. He will come in to apologize (though he's not sure what for), and if he seems contrite enough, we will make up. It's a crude system but it works.

"I'm sorry, honey," he said. "It's just that the game is on."

"You're right. Excuse me." I threw my hands up. "The game is *much* more important than your tired wife who's just had the worst day of her life at work. Don't let me interrupt you with my offensive presence."

Oh, I'm bad.

"But I just barely got home too," he said. "I just wanted to relax for a minute. It's the Utes."

"Great. And I'm sure the fact that you're ex-girlfriend is a cheerleader for them has nothing to do with your avid interest."

I'm *really* bad.

"What? Kelly?"

"Oh, so it's true." I wailed. "I knew it. Why don't you just divorce me already and go back to her if that's what you want so bad?"

I ran into the bedroom and slammed the door behind me.

I am the worst kind of person imaginable. And yet, I can't stop myself.

# Chapter 4

"How is it that you take longer than me?" I looked down at myself. "Am I still the girl here?"

"Babe, hold on," Mike whined. "I'm doing my hair."

The previous night's fight had lasted only an hour and all traces of it were forgotten as I leaned against the door frame of the bathroom, watching him.

I always laugh when he does his hair. I think it's the way he holds his arms up high over his head and looks at himself through lowered eyelids. Then he does this weird monkey dance where he sways a little while swooping an arm down and moving a piece of spiked hair this way; then, the other arm swoops down and moves another lock that way. Sway a little more. Swoop, swoop. Hold hands a few inches away from head at ear level. Turn left, turn right. Quick left again. Swoop. And done.

"Mike, we're going to be late for church again," I complained. "I hate walking into Relief Society late. I always think my mom's going to be in there waiting for me with a disapproving look."

"Your mom's not in our ward." He frowned at me in the mirror as he fumbled with his tie.

"It's a metaphor," I said impatiently. "A symbol. My mother is the symbol of my resistance to adulthood."

He stopped and looked at me over his shoulder.

"Obviously you've never taken Philosophy in Literature," I said, raising my chin just a tad.

He grunted and turned back to his tie.

I threw up my hands and stomped off.

*"Do you often react to Mike's use of time like that?" Dr. Farb taps his pen on his notebook.*

*"It's like he's this human black hole that sucks time into himself, and I'm this human hurricane that rushes through life, leaving a path of destruction in my wake." I tug at a strand of hair, growing annoyed at the many memories of impatiently waiting for Mike. "We do the same dance every time. Me, completely ready to go, pacing the house and checking his progress while tossing pointed remarks over my shoulder because I'm too much of a coward to look him in the eye and say, 'Oh, come on already. It's physically impossible to take as long as you do without trying.'"*

*"Do you think there's a possibility you might be transferring frustrations about other aspects of your life into these events?" Dr. Farb asks.*

*"What? You mean, like church?"*

*"If that's what you think I mean," Dr. Farb says. "Tell me about your feelings there."*

*"For one, I always feel, when I walk into Relief Society, like someone is going to point at me and scream, 'Wait! She doesn't belong here!' It's hard enough making the transition normally, but with the ward we live in . . ."*

*"What is upsetting about your current ward?" Dr. Farb asks.*

*"When we got engaged, Mike's boss's brother told us about this*

really great mother-in-law apartment in this really classy neighborhood that wasn't too expensive. We checked it out and fell in love with it." I laugh at myself, remembering how excited I was the first time I saw the apartment. "It was gorgeous. Vaulted ceilings, cream-colored walls, a walk-in closet—and only seven hundred dollars a month. Hello? I'll take two, please.

"And the neighborhood was beautiful. It was tucked away at the base of a mountain, and all the houses around us were at least half a million. We considered ourselves very lucky.

"What we didn't realize about our classy neighborhood was that simply living there did not grant you access to it," I say, my smile fading. "No one talked to us, introduced themselves, or even made eye contact. The closest we came to interaction with anyone was when the children of the families around us would look at us and grimace. Even the couple that we were renting the apartment from would only speak to us if absolutely necessary. We had tainted their perfect oasis because we were . . . poor. Shudder."

"So you feel out of place because of your economic background?"

"It's not just that. It's even in the way I see things. When you go to church, it's because you want to share experiences with like-minded people, but how can people pretend to care about you one day of the week and ignore your for the rest of it?"

"Have you ever let anyone in your ward know how their behavior has hurt you?" Dr. Farb asks.

"I don't even bother saying anything. I don't have the guts. Now, if I were Angel . . ."

"She's not afraid to speak her mind?"

"Angel's what I call a 'Hippie Mormon.' I think I'm one too, though certainly not as extreme. To stick with the same metaphor, I'm the bell-bottom-wearing, painted-flowers-on-the-face, sing-around-a-campfire kind. She's the sit-in-protesting, bra-burning, doesn't-shave-her-underarms kind. I wonder why Danny's ultraconservative mother doesn't like her? Hmm."

I watch as Dr. Farb writes something in his notebook. He glances up at me for a moment and then turns back to his writing.

*"I know what you're thinking. How can I believe so faithfully in a church where I obviously have some hostility? I look at it this way: The gospel is perfect. The people are not."*

*Dr. Farb glances back up at me but remains silent.*

*"Well, except me. I'm pretty awesome."*

As soon as Mike and I got back from church, I raced into the bedroom to change, having very little tolerance for skirts and high heels.

"Don't forget—dinner at my parents' tonight," I called to Mike as he collapsed on the couch and loosened his tie.

"Again?"

"Yes. They've begun scheduling them just to spite you."

"What's on the menu?"

"Shepherd's pie." I laughed.

"NO!" he wailed in mock horror.

I'm not sure where it came from or what purpose it serves, but shepherd's pie is an awful creation of my mother's that consists of corn, biscuit, some unidentified meat, mashed potatoes, and a few other things—the names of which I'm not sure. It's like taking an entire three-course meal, mixing it in a pan, and cooking it for forty-five minutes. This particular meal is one of the few things Mike and I have always agreed whole heartedly on: It is a perversion of nature.

Of course, we would never tell my mom this. She's got feelings, after all.

"It's probably not going to be that," I assured him. "She made it two weeks ago, and there's a rotation."

"Why don't you just call and ask?"

"Because I don't want to. Why don't you call?"

"I can't call; they're your family."

"Guffaw," I guffawed. "They like you more than me, and you know it. They never invited me to dinner before I met you. And I lived there."

"I guess we'll just have to be surprised, then."

"Guess so."

I should have called.

As soon as my little sister Rory answered the door, she gave me the look that was secret code for, "Mom made shepherd's pie."

I gave her the look that was code for, "Why didn't you stop her?" She gave me the look that was code for, "Has anyone ever stopped Mom—ever?" And I gave her the look that was code for, "Good point. But I did hear that once a Boy Scout stopped her from making black Jell-O with carrots in it for Halloween." I don't know if she was able to decode the entire message, though, because she just gave me a funny look and wandered off.

"You're fifteen minutes late," Mom said as I walked into the kitchen. She circled around the counter and hugged me.

"Sorry," I said, returning the hug. "It's Mike's fault. His hair wasn't behaving, or some other equally girly excuse."

Mom laughed. "Why don't you help Rory and Jeri set the table?"

"Is Lady coming?" I asked, looking around for any sign of her presence.

"Yeah. She's running late too, but she actually called to let us know." Mom handed me a stack of plates. "She's bringing that boyfriend of hers. Chance. What do you think of him?"

"Uh . . ." I quickly turned my back to her and began setting plates on the table. "He seems okay. Better than the last guy, right?"

"Does that mean you like him?" Mom asked. "Or not?"

"Lady's here. Just pulled up—and she's got that boy with her," Jeri announced.

I glanced up at the sound of my youngest sister's voice as she wandered into the room, nose in a book as usual.

"Why, Jericah Rose Wright. Don't you look all grown up today," I said, admiring her black skirt and pink button-up shirt. Jeri was the family's most devoted tomboy, making even church clothes look like proper tree-climbing ensembles. But that was not the Jeri standing before me. Her clothes were neatly ironed and still in place. In a few more years, she'd be turning boys into putty without even realizing it.

"She started Young Women today," Mom said. "I told you that."

"Oh, yeah." I nodded, remembering. "I forgot you just had your twelfth birthday. Did you like it?"

Jeri shrugged, briefly glancing up from her book. "I don't see what the big deal is."

"Shh," I warned. "Rory will hear you."

Jeri shrugged again and returned to her book.

A flurry of movement and noise at the door signaled Lady's entrance, her boyfriend in tow. Chance had come over a few times before but never for a family dinner. This was a highly personal gesture. It meant Lady was serious about the guy (as if moving in with him wasn't indication enough).

"Jeri! You look like a girl," Lady said, embracing her and laughing. Chance stood off to the side, hands deep in his pockets, a smile frozen on his face.

I turned to Lady and frowned, remembering her earlier confession. She was positively glowing. Maybe I was wrong. Maybe she's happy. Maybe moving in with Chance was good for her. Maybe I'm not as smart as I think I am. . . . Whoa, let's not start talking crazy talk here.

"Dinner's ready," Mom called out, setting a large dish in the center of the table and sweeping off the lid. "I experimented a little this time. Doesn't it smell great?"

Lady shot me the look that's code for, "Why didn't you stop her?" I gave her the look that's code for, "Has anyone ever stopped Mom—ever?" She might have shot me another look, but I had become distracted by something shiny.

After we all settled around the table, Dad asked Mike to bless the food. I snickered, remembering how Mike hated saying prayers in front of people. What? It's good for him.

"Guess who I ran into, today, Beth," Rory said, scooting the shepherd's pie away from her and toward me. I pushed it back.

Rory was fourteen and a miniature version of me, appearance-wise, though our personalities were very different.

"I don't know but I hope you apologized," I said.

"Huh?" she frowned while Mom and Dad chuckled and shook their heads at me. "Anyway, you'll never guess, so I'll just tell you—Elliot."

I let out a dramatic gasp and gripped my chest. Mike turned to me, concerned.

Rory was smart and talented, as well as moral, but in a way that didn't offend her peers. Everyone who knew her not only liked her but also respected her—a hard thing for any girl going through puberty to achieve, but she made it look effortless. I think I was equal parts proud and jealous of how easy she made life seem.

"Jeri, what did I say about reading at the table?" Mom asked, irritated.

"Sorry," Jeri mumbled, slipping her book off the table and onto her lap without looking up from it.

"Who's Elliot?" Mike asked.

"Elliot is Beth's ex-boyfriend's little brother." Rory was smug. I was confused.

"Why is this warranting a conversation?" I asked. "You see Elliot all the time. You go to school with him."

Mike lost interest in the conversation and began shoveling food into his mouth.

"Yeah, but this time when I saw him, he told me that Charlie is getting back from the Marines in a week," Rory said.

Mike lost interest in the food and began shoveling conversation into his ears.

"You're a troublemaker," I scolded, ignoring the fact that my heart had begun to pound and my cheeks were burning. "I'm telling your Mia Maid president on you."

"I *am* the Mia Maid president. You'll have to tell the secretary."

"Oh, she's making jokes now," I said, laughing and desperately trying to think of a way to redirect the conversation. "How's that going anyway?"

"It's fine, but—"

"Is this the ex that left for the Marines the day after he broke your heart, and you haven't seen him since? That one?" Mike asked.

Uh . . .

"Well, I . . . Lady's moving in with Chance."

"What?" Mom screeched, a piece of biscuit falling out of her mouth.

"Beth!" Lady gave me a look of shock and betrayal.

Okay, I did not handle that situation delicately.

"I mean, we . . . I," I stumbled, trying to think of the exact perfect thing to say for this situation. "I mean that she, uh . . . when I said 'move in' I meant that he was moving in on her, like in the sense that he was trying to date her. It's the new slang. Everyone's saying it, right, Rory?"

"Nice try." Rory laughed at me, enjoying the commotion my outburst was causing. Mom's eyes darted from me to Lady, her mouth still hanging open.

"Alright, everyone, settle down," Dad said calmly, the very voice of reason. "Let's finish our dinner, and then we'll talk this out. Nothing's going to change in half an hour."

"I can't eat now," Mom said, trying to hold back tears and throwing down her fork. "You come get me when you're done."

She stood up and stormed to her room, slamming the door. The only sounds following it were the gentle scrapes of forks against plates as everyone began to eat again—as slowly as they could.

# Chapter 5

*But whoso committeth adultery with a woman lacketh
understanding: he that doeth it destroyeth his own soul.
A wound and dishonor shall he get; and his reproach
shall not be wiped away.*

—Proverbs 6:32–33

"AND CHARLIE WAS THE *serious boyfriend you had right before you
met Mike?" Dr. Farb asks, flipping through his notes.*

*"I don't know if you could call it serious if only one of us took it
seriously."*

*I let out a harsh laugh to hide the bitterness of my remark.*

*"What do you mean by that? Did you feel like Charlie didn't
take the relationship as seriously as you did?" Dr. Farb clasps his
hands and rests his chin on them.*

*"What do you mean, 'did I feel'? I knew. It was a pretty hard
clue to miss. Here I was, thinking we were this perfect happy couple."
My voice rises and I gesture wildly. "Yeah, we had our problems, but
nothing I couldn't handle—then bam! 'Breaking news. The person
you think you know is not the person you actually know. We now
return you to your regularly scheduled programming.'"*

*Dr. Farb picks up his pen and makes a note. "Would you care to
elaborate on the specific incident when he broke your trust?"*

"It was in May. What, two years ago, now? I was on my way to Charlie's apartment when he called my cell to tell me he was running late. He said I should just let myself in and he'd be there in about ten minutes," I say. "No big deal. We'd been dating for over a year and half and I spent as much time at his apartment as anywhere else. When I walked in, I looked around to see if Owen was home."

"And Owen is?"

"Oh, that's his roommate. The last time I'd been over, Charlie and I were hanging out in the living room, and Owen had wandered in without a shirt on. He was furious with Charlie for not telling him I was over. Both Owen and I were very embarrassed; Charlie thought it was hilarious."

Dr. Farb makes another note and nods for me to continue.

"Anyway, I decided a repeat of that incident would be worse without Charlie present, so I went to his bedroom to wait.

"I remember sitting on his bed and looking around, wondering what I could do to amuse myself for a few minutes. There was this book on his dresser. The room was littered with books since Charlie was a great academic, but something about this particular book caught my eye. I think because it was new. When I picked it up, a picture fell out. It was a photo of Charlie and some girl. They had their arms around each other and they were laughing."

I stop talking and sigh, blinking hard. Dr. Farb looks at me with concern but does not speak.

"I remember thinking, 'Was this a previous girlfriend? Why had he never mentioned her?' But when I looked closer at the picture, I noticed that he was wearing the watch I'd bought him for Christmas."

"That doesn't necessarily mean he was cheating," Dr. Farb points out.

"That's what I thought," I say, annoyed that Dr. Farb wasn't giving my deductive reasoning more credit. "There had to be some explanation. She was a cousin or a good friend. A very, very good friend. But then I opened the book to the front cover. The entire page was an inscription, written in pink pen with lots of loops and hearts above the i's instead of dots. I hate it when girls do that.

"As I read it, I sank down to the floor—tears were running down my face and something like shock or denial was setting in." I lean forward, resting my head on my knees, my voice becoming muffled. "I remember single sentences jumping out at me, my eyes burning as I read and reread: 'Ten long months of dating . . . Been through so much . . . Never forget the time we stayed up all night watching the stars . . . Love, Scarlet . . . Love, Scarlet . . . Love, Scarlet . . . Love—'"

I sniff loudly and lift my head, avoiding Dr. Farb's steady gaze.

"I felt more than heard Charlie walk in. When I looked up, he was standing in the doorway and just staring down at me, expressionless. I asked him if it was true. His response?" I snorted and mimicked Charlie's voice. "'Which part?' So I just threw down the book and left."

"And was that the end of it?" Dr. Farb asks.

"Yeah. About a week later, a mutual friend told me he'd left for the Marines. I remember feeling only relief. Relief that I would have no opportunity to try to work things out."

# Chapter 6

"ANGEL? THIS BETTER BE good. I was about to win an argument."

I shrugged at Mike in apology for answering my cell phone in the middle of his sentence.

We were on our Tuesday-night date at Albertsons, rehashing our usual food-related arguments. I don't look through the expiration dates enough. He buys more fruit than he can eat. No more Doritos because they make my breath smell. No more ice cream because it gives him gas. We were in the middle of my brand-name-versus-generic speech when the cell phone had interrupted his rebuttal.

"It's gone too far," she exclaimed. "I can't do this anymore. I can't take it, Beth, I can't take it, I tell you!"

"And what has brought you to contemplation of suicide this time?" I held up a bag of chocolate doughnuts to Mike. He nodded and I tossed them into our cart.

"Danny," Angel said. "He's gone too far with this budgeting stuff."

Of course. Danny loves to budget. He loves to budget like Mike loves to watch basketball or like I love to talk. He's got separate credit cards for gas, monthly bills, emergencies, groceries, entertainment . . . there are more, I just can't remember them all. What Danny has a hard time budgeting for is his wife.

"What did he do?" I asked, browsing the brightly colored boxes of food in front of me. I picked one up and examined it.

Their last money-related argument was because she wanted to buy a four-dollar notebook that she thought was cute. He gave her a lecture about whether she thought the notebook was a necessary item or a luxury item. Usually I don't get involved in these things, but homeboy went too far when he told her that KFC was not a necessary item. KFC is always necessary.

"He wouldn't let me buy Cap'n Crunch," she wailed.

I raised my eyebrows in surprise and looked back down at the box in my hand. Cap'n Crunch.

"He said it was a luxury food item, and we were at the store only to buy necessary food items," she continued. "Who says 'food item' anyway? I mean, who talks like that?"

"But . . . it's Cap'n Crunch," I said, tossing the box of cereal into my cart with an unusual amount of satisfaction.

"See, Danny?" Her voice was muffled for a moment. "Beth agrees with me."

"Is he right there?" I asked.

"Yeah."

"You're saying all of this, and he's right there?"

"So?"

I shook my head and laughed. "So, what happened?"

"Well, I pointed out to him that at the time of his complaint we had no less than ten cans of Dinty Moore Beef Stew. All of them for him. I said if he could have ten cans of Dinty Moore Beef Stew then I could have Cap'n Crunch. He said that it didn't count because the stew was for his lunch, and I said that the cereal was for my breakfast, so what was the difference?"

"Uh-huh." Mike was giving me the look that signaled I was pacing while on the phone again. He hates when I do that. I stopped, planting my feet firmly beside the cart.

"He said that if I had to get it, I should get the generic brand, and I tried to explain that for Cap'n Crunch, generic brand doesn't cut it, you know? But whatever. So I took everything that was mine out of the cart and put it back on the shelf. Taught him a lesson."

"Didn't he try to stop you?" I started pacing again.

"Oh, we were already in line by then. The lady at the register had started ringing us up and there were people behind us. He was stuck."

"Ah, brilliant." The cell phone beeped, and I glanced at the caller ID. JoJo's name flashed across the screen. "Angel—that's JoJo. I've been trying to get ahold of her forever, so I've got to take this."

"Fine," Angel grumbled. "Toss me aside like so much dirty laundry. Doesn't matter that my marriage is falling apart."

"Anj—it was Cap'n Crunch."

"Now you're just minimizing."

"Whatever. I'll call you later." I laughed. "And remember, Angel, you've got your whole lives to make each other miserable. Don't overexert yourselves in the first few months."

I clicked over and glanced at Mike, who was pouting, obviously annoyed that I was now on another phone call.

"JoJo! How are you?" I asked in a rush. "I keep trying to call you. I feel like the socially awkward preteen who can't take a hint."

"I know and I'm sorry." JoJo's voice sounded far away. "I've just been so busy with school and Ted and stuff."

"Yeah, I understand," I assured her, shaking my head at a can of extra spicy bean dip Mike was holding up. None of that in my house while we only have one bathroom. "Anyway, I was thinking we should have a girl's night. You, me, Angel. I could see what Lady's up to. It'll be great."

"Oh, I don't know," JoJo said. "I'd have to talk to Ted first.

What would we be doing? I probably shouldn't stay out too late, you know?"

"Right." I laughed, though I was starting to feel like I was at a dentist's office—and I was the dentist pulling teeth. "We could do whatever. It doesn't matter."

"I could kick your butt at pool like I always do," she suggested.

"Oh, trash talk," I said with relief. "I see how it is. You know I was letting you win, right?"

"Uh-huh," she said. I heard the slamming of a door and a man's voice yelling something in the background. "Oh, Ted's home. I'vegottagoI'llcallyoulaterbye."

"Bye." I was talking to dead air. She'd already hung up.

I stared at my phone for a minute, and then threw it back in my purse.

"That was weird," I said as much to Mike as to myself.

"What was?" he asked, holding up two bags of chips. I pointed to the Ruffles.

"JoJo. She just sounded . . . weird. It was probably my imagination. Forget I said anything."

"Oh, shoot, we've got to hurry," Mike said, glancing at his watch. "The Utes are playing."

"No, seriously, Mike, forget I said anything," I muttered under my breath as I followed him to the check stand.

# Chapter 7

*In a world of turmoil and uncertainty, it is more
important than ever to make our families the center
of our lives and the top of our priorities.*

—L. Tom Perry, "The Importance of Family,"
*Ensign,* May 2003, 40

"I'M HEARING SOME NEGATIVITY *toward the dynamic of your family.
Where do you think that's coming from?" Dr. Farb asks, tapping his
pen on his notebook.*

*"What? What are you talking about? I love my family." I cross
my arms over my chest, offended.*

*"That's not what I said." Dr. Farb straightens in his seat and
pushes up his glasses. "I've noticed that when we talk about your
family—more specifically your parents—you change the subject. Are
you holding something back that you would like to share?"*

*"No. No, I'm not having any problems with my parents, so that's
why . . . I don't want to waste this time talking about something I
don't even have a problem with."*

*Dr. Farb watches me, his mouth pressed into a firm line.*

*"What? Are you expecting me to whine about my first dad? You
think that I should be upset because he never wanted to be a part of
my life? Or because when my Mom got remarried, she popped out*

brand-spanking-new daughters like she was trying to start over so she could get it right the second time?"

The memories connected with what I am saying flash before me and I blink back angry tears. "Or how every time I tried to impress my stepdad, I would fall flat on my face? Like when I joined softball but got cut, so they signed me up for tee-ball and I still stunk up the place? Do you know what tee-ball is? It's a little ball on a stick. It's sitting there motionless, waiting—begging to be hit by the bat, and I still missed it!"

I hear my voice rising, and I pause, taking a deep breath.

"So you were receiving the message that you weren't worthy of your parents' love?" Dr. Farb asks.

"No. That's not what I'm saying. You're twisting my words." I lean toward Dr. Farb, my fists clenched.

"So you believe your parents are proud of you?"

"Of course they are. I did everything right. I got good grades, dated good guys, hung out with a good crowd. I helped babysit my younger sisters. And I even got married in the temple. I mean, for any Mormon family, there's no topping that. And, honestly, I'm pretty sure my stepdad likes Mike more than he likes me."

I let out a loud laugh, but Dr. Farb's face is expressionless as he stares at me. What is with that infuriating stare?

"It was a joke. I know my stepdad loves me."

"Do you?" Dr. Farb flips to a new page in his notebook.

"I mean, look at Lady. She did drugs, snuck out, mouthed off . . . next to her, I'm the perfect daughter."

"Do you feel like it's a competition?"

I shoot him a look and shrug.

"If it is, I'm winning in the good-behavior/fade-into-the-wall-paper round, and she's got the gold in general-attention/time-spent-on-her round."

"It sounds like you resent the amount of time your older sister gets from your parents," Dr. Farb says.

"No, I'm just kidding. Trying to lighten the mood. Why do we have to take everything so seriously?"

Dr. Farb frowns and flips through his notebook. "You've made a lot of jokes throughout this session, Bethany. Do you have a hard time taking things seriously?"

"No. I just have a good sense of humor. I know how to laugh at life."

"Those are good qualities," Dr. Farb assures me. "But it is just as valuable to know when things should not be made into a joke."

"I know that."

"Okay. I would like you to tell me about a memory from your past. Pick an especially powerful one, and don't make any jokes while you share this memory with me." Dr. Farb poises his pen above the notebook and watches me expectantly.

"Okay. I can do this . . . Oh, I know." I say, clapping my hands together. "When I was in second grade, I still had a bad habit of sucking my thumb. I would always do it when I thought no one was watching. During that time in my life, I was kind of awkward.

"I didn't really fit in with the kids. I wore hand-me-down clothes and had stringy hair, so I was teased a lot. The day after Halloween was particularly painful. I found myself walking down the hall alone, so I stole a few seconds to suck my thumb for comfort. All of a sudden, I hear this voice beside me saying, 'Waa. I'm a baby. I suck my thumb. Waa.' I turn to see this girl in a wheelchair rolling by. I was so embarrassed."

"Very good, Bethany. See? That wasn't so hard." Dr. Farb congratulates me.

"Yeah. I just remember thinking, 'Wow, I must be a loser. Even the special-needs kids are making fun of me.'"

# Chapter 8

"You're talking to me again?" My voice brimmed with hope as I answered my phone. I turned to Mike, but he stared at the television, completely unaware that I was even there.

Lady let out a loud sniffle and whimpered something on the other end of the phone line.

After my outburst on Sunday, Lady and Mom fought for the better part of an hour, eventually collapsing into tears and hugs. Chance had slipped away unnoticed in the midst of the commotion, and everyone else just watched with barely contained amusement. When I approached Lady for my reconciliatory hug, I was given a dirty look instead.

"What? Lady? I can't hear you." I glanced at my cell phone to check the reception. "Lady?"

"Chance didn't come home last night," she said, followed by another loud sniffle.

"Oh, honey! Are you okay? Do you want me to come over?"

"No . . . but can I come over to your place? Are you home?"

"Yeah. Of course." I looked around my apartment, deciding it was presentable enough for a visitor. Of course, I'd have to clean Mike off of the couch, but I'd leave him be until Lady got here.

"Are you sure?"

"Lady. Get your butt over here."

Before I even had the sentence fully out, there was a knock at my door. When I opened it, Lady stood there, clutching her cell phone and a handful of tissues.

"What?" She asked as I stood in front of her, one eyebrow raised.

"Nothing." I opened the door wider. "Come in, come in."

"Hey, Mike," Lady said to Mike, who continued to stare at the television, so absorbed in his basketball game that he gave no indication of having heard her.

I walked over and stood directly in front of the television. "Mike, honey. Can you go watch basketball in the bedroom? I need to talk to Lady."

"Babe!" he whined. I didn't budge, and he realized that if he wanted to catch any more of the game, he'd better give in. He leapt off the couch and bounded into the bedroom, briefly nodding at Lady as he swept by her.

I flipped off the television and sat down on the couch, motioning for Lady to join me.

"Okay, tell me everything," I said, taking a deep breath and preparing for the worst.

"Chance wanted to go to this party at Guy's house—you know? The one with the overbite. But I was feeling kind of sick." Lady put her hand on her stomach and rubbed it. "I think I'm coming down with the stomach flu or something. So I told him to just go without me . . ."

"And he didn't come home?" I asked.

"Yeah. He still isn't home, as far as I know." She wiped at her nose with a tissue. "It started getting really late so at, like, one in the morning I called Guy, but no one answered. Then I started to get *really* worried, and I just kept calling and calling; I didn't know what else to do."

"I understand," I cooed.

"Finally, after I'd called, like, five times, this girl answered and I asked if she knew who Chance was, and she said yes . . . and the way she said it—I don't know. Made me really uncomfortable. So I asked if I could talk to him and she said he wasn't there."

"Really?"

"So I asked if she knew where he went or if he'd, like, tried to drive drunk or something." She was talking faster and struggling for breath. "And she said all she knew was that he'd left with a couple of girls and another guy a few hours ago."

"Wow." I rubbed her back in an attempt to calm her down. "What are you going to do?"

"I don't know." She collapsed into tears. "Oh, Beth! I don't know what to do."

"Maybe you should take things back a step," I said, shamelessly pushing my own agenda. "Maybe you could move out and just try dating casually or something."

"You don't understand." Lady hunched over, looking dejected. "I know I shouldn't have moved in. I know I shouldn't be living like this, but I—I just can't control myself."

"Has he ever done anything like this before?"

"I don't know." She paused, thinking. "I mean, I never lived with him before. I don't know what he may have been doing after I'd go home."

"You know Mom would let you move back in with her in a heartbeat," I suggested.

"No," she gasped. "I'd rather just work things out with Chance."

"*Lady,*" I pleaded.

"It could be worse," Lady reasoned. "My friend, Shelly—her boyfriend cheats on her. And Jenny's boyfriend calls her names and makes her change her clothes if she doesn't look the way he wants her to. Chance would never do that to me."

"No, he just goes off all night without bothering to let you know where he is or what he's doing," I said. "Yeah, you've really got it good."

"We can't all have our perfect little lives arranged like you do." Lady rolled her eyes.

"Don't you think you deserve someone who makes you happy? For real?" I asked. "Yeah, Mike and I have our moments, but I know he's got my back. I know he'd never intentionally hurt me. You don't think you deserve that?"

"Weren't you just complaining the other night that Mike doesn't pay attention to you anymore?"

"So?" I stood and put my hands on my hips. "I'm not saying my relationship is perfect. No relationship is. But at least I'm not running to your house desperate and upset because Mike disappeared on me."

"You sound just like Mom." Lady jumped up and threw her bag over her shoulder. "You're not as perfect as you think you are, and you've made your share of mistakes, so don't stand there and tell me how I need to live."

"Are you serious?" I asked, following her into the entryway. "You're living with a guy you barely like, who—let's face it—is kind of a jerk, and you don't want to move out because what? Mom might be right? The mess you're in is your own fault, and the sooner you realize that, the sooner you can get it together."

"I don't live like you do. I don't make decisions the way you do." Lady shook her head in disgust. "You think you're so perfect, so much better than us little people who can't get our acts together like you did. Are you even happy? Or are you still just trying to be perfect for Mom?"

"What! I—"

"You're so terrified of doing something wrong that . . . that you're not even, like, *alive* anymore."

Before I could say more, she was out the door, slamming it behind her.

Mike poked his head out of the bedroom. "Is everything okay? Things didn't sound so good from in here."

"I don't know," I said, walking back into the living room and falling onto the couch. "I suck."

"Baby." He came out of the bedroom and sat down on the couch. "What happened? Are you okay?"

"I'm so tired of worrying about her all the time, and feeling responsible for her," I sighed. "Why can't I just live her life for her?"

"Then it wouldn't be her life anymore, would it?" he said, wrapping his arms around me.

"Just for a little while. Just so I could straighten it out."

"I know it's hard, babe." He pulled back and looked into my eyes. "But part of growing up is learning that most times, all we can do is be there for the people we love. No matter how much we want to change things for them."

"Stop it," I said.

"What?"

"Doing that." I put my head on his shoulder. "I thought I was the smart one in the relationship."

"Does that mean I'm the pretty one?"

I laughed. "No. You're the lucky one. For getting me."

"I am." His voice was soft, and I snuggled closer, deciding a clever reply would ruin the moment.

# Chapter 9

I WAS WORRIED ABOUT Lady, but it was my conversation with JoJo that, however brief, lingered with me long after she'd hung up. It wasn't just that she'd sounded nervous or stressed out—everyone has their moments. It was something else in her voice. . . . Fear? Desperation? Isolation?

"You're just being dramatic," Mike said after I had called him at work a few days later to ask for his opinion. "Just because she's too busy to drop everything to talk to you."

"Wow. Thanks, Mike. You've really put things into perspective for me. How could I have confused my overwhelming ego with concern for my friend?"

"I didn't mean it like that. Stop twisting my words."

I tightened my grip on the cell phone, imagining it was his neck. "I'm trying to figure out what's wrong with my friend, and you're just being flippant about it."

There was a pause. "What does 'flippant' mean again?"

"It means you're a jerk."

This pause was longer. I glanced at the screen of my phone. The pause stretched on for almost a minute.

"Hello?" I asked.

"You shouldn't call me names," he said, genuinely hurt. "I never call you names."

"Well, that's because that is what's expected of you. You're the nice guy and I'm the harpy." How dare he tell me not to call him names. And "*jerk?*" That wasn't even as bad as some of the ones I was now considering. "You're just as rude to me as I am to you, but you're all politically correct about it so I can't point it out as easily."

"That doesn't even make sense." His voice got louder. "All I said was that you're probably making a bigger deal out of this than it is. You'll find out JoJo is just fine and feel like an idiot for jumping to a bunch of conclusions."

"Wait a minute," I said. "You just called me an idiot after throwing a fit about me calling you a jerk."

"I didn't call you an idiot," he explained. "I said you would *feel* like an idiot."

"That's exactly what I'm talking about." I stomped my foot so hard it shot stabs of pain up my leg. "You throw in a few safety words so you can call me any name you want and get away with it."

There was another pause.

I could hear muffled voices.

"Mike?"

No response.

"Mike."

"Yeah, uh, what? Sorry, babe. Jim was talking to me."

I let out a frustrated growl and slammed my phone shut, then considered throwing it across the room. I decided that any satisfaction derived from it would pale in comparison to the inconvenience and cost of breaking it, so I slipped off my shoe and threw that instead.

*That hits the spot,* I thought as I slipped off my other shoe, deciding it should meet with the same fate and glancing around my apartment for anything else I could throw.

"Beth, I need you and I need you now," a voice yelled through my door, accompanied by loud banging. "Beth. Beth, Beth, Bethbethbethbethbeth."

"Wow, calm down," I called out, dropping the shoe and opening the door. "Sheesh, Angel. I've already got enough of a reputation around this neighborhood without future psych patients screaming my name."

She pushed past me, out of breath and looking ill.

"What's wrong?" My sarcasm fell away as concern took over.

"I . . . have . . . to . . . have . . ."

"What?"

"Lunch," Angel breathed heavily. "With my mother-in-law. By myself. She wants to—oh, I can't say it, it's too horrible."

I stifled a laugh and adopted an expression of anxiousness. "What is it, Angel? What does she want to do to you?"

"She wants to bond."

"Isn't that a good thing?" I asked as if talking to a small child.

"No." Angel looked at me as if she were shocked at my stupidity. "It's a *trick*."

"Ah."

"That's why I came here."

"Huh?"

"I have to meet her in half an hour, and here's the plan." She glanced at her watch and then looked me up and down. "You're going to change and come with me. I'll just say something like I had plans with you and couldn't break them; or I ran into you in the parking lot or something. I don't know—just get changed. Now."

I shrugged and followed her into my bedroom. I decided I could use a good distraction, and with Angel's flair for the dramatic, the event would be anything but unremarkable. She held up a few shirts and finally tossed one at me, followed by a pair of pants and shoes—the last item hitting me hard in the stomach and causing me to wonder if inanimate objects could exact revenge. Next time I felt like throwing something, I'd make sure it was soft.

"So, does this mean you're buying?" I asked a few moments later as we sped down the freeway in her car.

"I'll buy you a pony for doing this," Angel swore, switching lanes and cutting off a red Volvo, and then switching back. I watched her, wishing I'd offered to drive. I looked at her closer. Was she sweating? Wow, she was in worse shape than I thought.

"What's the deal with this lunch thing, anyway?" I asked. "She's never wanted to hang out with you before."

"I know," Angel said, speeding by a cop and slamming on her brakes after spotting him in her rearview mirror. "I think Danny said something to her, but he won't fess up. All I know is that she calls me this morning and is all gooey sweet, saying that she never gets to spend any 'girl time' with me and that she was free for lunch if I was. What could I say? She caught me totally off guard."

"You're probably making a bigger deal of this than it is," I said. *Did I just quote Mike? Ick.*

"Ha. Double ha. It's a test. It's a test, I just know it." Angel was the kind of girl who used to have bad dreams in high school about forgetting everything that was on a test the night before she was supposed to take it.

"Okay," I said. "It is a huge deal. This is the moment on which your entire future hinges. If you don't get this right, everything—*everything* will be destroyed."

"Shut up," she said, laughing. "You really suck at making people feel better, you know? Remember what you said to me at my grandma's funeral?"

"Uh . . ." I was seventeen when her grandmother died. I had no idea what I said to her.

"You said, 'Wow, she's not as dead-looking as I thought she'd be.' Remember?" Angel was laughing so hard she swerved the car into the next lane.

I grabbed onto the door, bracing myself. "Well, it was the first time I'd seen a dead body. I didn't know what to expect."

"It was so funny. Everyone was standing around her coffin crying and sniffing—even me, and you come up and just look at her." As Angel was saying this she was waving her arms toward the imaginary coffin—which was nowhere near the steering wheel. "And blah—out comes that sentence. No one knew what to do, and you had no idea that what you'd said was so . . . so . . ."

"Stupid?"

"Yeah." Angel's hands were now back on the steering wheel. "I knew my grandma was sitting there laughing her head off. And it, I don't know, just made me feel better."

"So you want me to tell your mother-in-law she's not as dead-looking as I thought she'd be?" I asked helpfully.

"If you say *that,* I'll buy you two ponies."

Angel pulled into the parking lot of Olive Garden, stealing a spot from a blue minivan. She turned off the ignition and stared out the windshield, frozen. I watched her for a moment; then I handed her an old Wendy's paper bag I found on the floor beneath my feet. She grabbed it and put it to her mouth, breathing in deeply. Coughing, she threw the bag down and pulled a fry out of her mouth.

"You couldn't check to see if the bag was empty?"

"Sorry," I said, not bothering to hide my laughter.

She tossed the fry at me and got out of the car, pausing to fix her hair in the reflection of the driver side window.

"Twenty bucks says she's already in there, seated, and impatiently awaiting our arrival," Angel muttered as we walked in.

"But we're right on time," I said, glancing at my watch.

"Hello. Welcome to Olive Garden. Just two today?" A short blonde girl with the most annoyingly perfect skin asked.

"Uh, there's actually a third person we're supposed to meet," Angel said, searching the nearby tables for her mother-in-law.

"What's the name?"

"I, uh, her name is Janice," Angel said. "I'm Angel."

The blonde scanned her clipboard. "Oh, yes. Follow me, please."

Our journey lasted no more than three short steps to a booth on our left. Janice, whose back was to us, glanced up from her menu as the blonde motioned us to our seats.

"Angel, I'm glad you made it," she said, sliding her eyes to me. "And you brought Beth."

"Oh, yeah. About that," Angel said, all smiles and good humor. "It was the funniest thing. On the way here, Beth called me because her car was out of gas and stopped on the side of the road. I had to swing by and pick her up, but I didn't want to be late for our lunch, so I just invited her along."

"Well, that's so thoughtful of you," Janice said, matching Angel's good humor and raising her one gushing compliment. "Beth, aren't you lucky to have such a thoughtful friend?"

"So lucky," I murmured. "Don't know how I got so darn lucky."

"You should try the Chicken and Portobello Mushroom Alfredo," Janice confided. "It's delicious."

"Mmm," Angel said with just a touch too much enthusiasm.

"So, Danny tells me you're working on a CD?" Janice asked.

"Just a sample one that I can send to some record companies," Angel said. She'd been playing piano and writing songs since she was fourteen and, in my opinion, was destined for stardom. I think that's actually the only reason I'm friends with her. She promised to buy me a boat when she made it. Hey, that means I'll be getting a boat *and* a pony. Yay for me.

"Hm," she said, looking down at her napkin, which she kept straightening on her lap. "That's a really fun hobby, I'm sure, but what about when you start having children?"

I could feel Angel stiffen beside me.

"Lots of successful musicians have a solid family life," I jumped in. "Sarah McLachlan, Tori Amos, Chris Martin—"

"Danny and I have already discussed that," Angel cut in. "And we decided we'd tackle that obstacle when we came to it. Suffice it to say, my children will always come first, but I don't think it's the type of thing where I'd have to choose one or the other."

"Of course, honey," Janice said, patting Angel's hand. "But aren't you worried about the lifestyle? Is that the kind of environment you want to raise children in?"

"What kind of environment are we talking about?" Angel asked. I could tell she was starting to lose it, so I pinched her leg under the table to remind her to hold it together.

"You know," Janice whispered, smiling at our waitress as she put our drinks and a basket of bread down in front of us. "*Drugs, sex, greed . . .*"

I shook my head at the waitress to let her know we weren't ready to order and turned back to the conversation.

"I think those things are a danger no matter what profession you choose," Angel said, taking a deep breath to calm herself and forcing out a laugh. "It's just more publicized if you're famous. Besides, I want to use my music to spread the Lord's message. That's why I've been given this gift from him."

"Oh." Janice looked visibly relieved. "You're going to be doing Christian rock."

Uh-oh. Angel hated Christian rock. She'd just had a fight with Danny about it because he kept trying to get her into it, but she thought it was too cheesy and in-your-face. Angel was more subtle and wanted to use that fact to appeal to a larger audience, the people whom she felt needed the message more but wouldn't listen to anything so overtly Christian.

"Hey, how's Rose doing these days?" I asked in a desperate attempt to redirect the conversation. Rose was Janice's youngest, and at seventeen, was always up to something worth talking about. "I hear she's got a new boyfriend?"

"She did," Janice said, turning back to her menu. "But she had to break up with him."

"Oh, that's too bad," I said, pushing the change of topic. "What happened?"

Angel began glancing through her menu as well, regaining color in her cheeks.

"Well, it was nothing really. They weren't that serious to begin with, but . . . did you know that his parents are divorced?"

My stomach dropped. *Abort. Abort.* Angel's head shot up.

"No, I didn't," I said, forcing the words out.

"And you know how it is," Janice said. "It's a psychological fact that people from broken homes have more emotional problems than other people. Imagine what kind of a father he'd make. I'm glad that Rose was smart enough to see that it was a waste of time once I pointed that out to her."

"Janice." Angel spit the word out. "Did you know that Beth's mom got divorced? The man you met was her stepdad."

*That'll do it for me.* I laughed nervously at Janice's shocked look and excused myself to the ladies' room. I would've been just fine with Angel not mentioning that little fact. I'm not sure if she said it to defend me or to back Janice into a corner, and I didn't really care.

"Excuse me." I stopped a waitress a few feet away. "Where are the bathrooms?"

"Just down that hall, first right," she called over her shoulder, rushing off.

As I made my way down the aisle, I felt a hand grab my wrist.

"Beth? Bethany, is that you?"

I froze, afraid to turn.

Still staring straight ahead, I cleared my throat. "Hey, Charlie. It's been a while."

"Yeah." He paused. I still refused to look at him. "Why don't you sit down for a sec? We've got a lot of catching up to do . . . you look great."

I don't know why, but I turned and slid into the seat across from him, finally meeting his gaze. This was so familiar it was eerie, sitting across from him, looking into his eyes. I hadn't seen Charlie in over a year, and our last night together had not ended well.

He looked back at me, his brown eyes soft and concerned. I looked down, trying not to notice how his face had thinned, making him look stronger and more handsome. His hair was shorter, too, but still dark and full. My eyes flicked over to his fingers as they tapped the table; they were long and graceful, just like I remembered.

"I hear you're married now," Charlie said, picking up the glass in front of him and taking a drink.

"Yeah." I fingered my wedding ring.

"Congratulations."

"Thanks." I looked around. "Are you here by yourself?"

"No," he said, leaning back. "I'm here with an old friend. They're in the bathroom."

"Owen?"

"No."

"What's he up to these days?"

"He's got a girlfriend, now. She seems nice. I think he's going to marry her."

"That's great," I said, genuinely pleased. I'd always had a soft spot for Owen.

There was an awkward pause.

"So, I guess you just got back?"

"Yeah, a few days ago." He looked down at his hands and then back up at me. "So . . . how are you? Are you happy?"

"What? I mean, yes. Yes, very happy."

My heart was pounding, and I felt equal parts guilty for being here and an uncomfortable sort of longing to go back to something I could never go back to.

"It was kind of fast, don't you think?" he asked, no longer attempting to be unfamiliar. "I mean, I was only gone a little over a year."

"What does that have to do with anything?" I swallowed back my anger. "Do you think if I wasn't married, you'd have any kind of chance?"

He seemed taken aback by this and didn't respond.

"I should probably go," I said, rising. "This isn't appropriate and I—"

"Wait, no. I'm sorry. Sit back down. Please," he said. I melted back into the seat. "So, what are you doing now? Still working at that clothing store?"

"No." I laughed despite myself. "That was awful. No, I work at Barnes and Noble now."

"That's great; which one?"

"The one just around the corner." I stopped, almost saying: *The one we always used to go to.*

Charlie nodded as if he'd heard the unspoken part.

"We should get together sometime," he said. I began to shake my head, but he rushed on. "I mean you and your husband. I'd really like to meet him."

"Yeah, I don't think that's going to happen." I could just imagine asking Mike if he'd mind if my ex-boyfriend stopped by for a visit. Which one? The one that mangled your heart? The one you never resolved your feelings for? Yeah, sounds great; what time?

He looked disappointed and said something softly.

"What?" I asked, leaning closer.

"I really miss you." He caught my gaze and held it.

"I've really got to get going now," I said, out of breath, moving in slow motion. I slid out of the seat and walked away, letting his husky "good-bye" fall behind me.

I hadn't done anything wrong, so why did I feel so guilty?

# Chapter 10

*It is certain that almost any good man and any good woman can have happiness and a successful marriage if both are willing to pay the price.*

—Spencer W. Kimball, *Marriage and Divorce*

"Before Mike and I were married, I had a couple of panic attacks," I say, twisting my hands in my lap. "I mean, I saw myself stumbling into my future with my childhood becoming farther away and harder to remember.

"When I lined up the kids I knew against the adults I knew, guess which group was having more fun? This caused me, on a variety of occasions and in no particular order, to postpone, rearrange, or cancel the wedding. I don't know why he put up with it . . . I guess because he really loved me. Had I been him, I would've dumped my butt long ago."

Dr. Farb chuckles. "Could you describe one of these 'panic attacks' for me?"

I frown at him and fold my arms across my chest. I know this is therapy and all, but what's with the questions? That whole last tirade is in answer to a question. Where's the part where he starts telling me what's wrong with me?

"Sure." I sigh in resignation. "The last one happened after a fight—I think it had something to do with him expecting me to actually prepare meals for him once we were married, or maybe it was the time he called me 'forehead,' in reference to, well . . . my giant forehead. I can't remember.

"Anyway, I cancelled the wedding and went out for a girls' night with JoJo. When I got home, I found Mike in my parents' living room, a plate of heart-shaped chocolate chip cookies in his hand. Apparently, he'd come over three hours earlier to talk things out, but since I wasn't home, he ended up pouring his heart out to my mom, telling her how much he loved me and didn't want to lose me."

"It sounds like he was very dedicated to the relationship," Dr. Farb observes.

"Dedicated? I challenge any girl in the world to say no to that guy. Maybe I wasn't ready to get married. Maybe I should have waited before taking the plunge, but the cold, hard fact is I didn't. I couldn't. I mean, he was perfect."

"So, you believe he's perfect?" Dr. Farb asks, looking at me over the top of his glasses.

"Not literally, of course." I roll my eyes. "But pretty close. I mean, before we met, he used to party a lot. He drank about every day. Kind of took a hiatus from Church, if you know what I mean. When we started dating and I found some beer in his fridge, I told him that it wasn't anything against him, but I simply don't date men who drink. I said I wasn't trying to make him feel guilty or to, you know, change him, but that there's enough people in the world for us to both get what we want. He threw the beer out and said that I was what he wanted, and he'd been meaning to quit anyway. Smooth, huh?"

# Chapter 11

I WAS NURSING A hot cocoa, thinking about my ex-boyfriend and watching a ridiculous romantic comedy, which was full of what Angel likes to call "love propaganda."

John Cusack was in the process of overcoming various obstacles to reunite with his true love, Kate Beckinsale. A misunderstanding ensues, and it seems that all is lost. But wait, no—they manage to find each other again despite fate and a spunky ex-girlfriend.

He performed some variation of the "look at how I've overcome various obstacles to reunite with you, despite fate and my spunky ex-girlfriend" line. I tossed a pillow at the screen.

"Oh, isn't that sweet?" I muttered to myself. "But what are you going to do when he stinks up the bathroom right before you've got to get ready for work? Huh? Or when he can't complete a conversation with you because every five minutes he's taking a call from his boss? Or what . . . what about when the former love of your life comes back, wishing he could have a second chance? Where's the romantic background music then?"

*Okay. Okay, I'm talking to myself . . . worse, I'm talking to the television set. I'm going to need a lot more chocolate.*

My cell phone rang and I fell off the couch reaching for it. I flipped it open, still dizzy as I tried to pick myself up.

"Hello?" I managed before I dropped the phone again. I stumbled but grabbed it without hanging up. "Hello, hello?"

"Beth? Honey, are you okay?"

"Mike." I smiled and held the phone out lovingly, kissing it. "I love you, baby. You know that, don't you?"

"Okay." He laughed. "Well, I was just calling to see if you wanted me to bring something home for dinner."

He was *so* sweet. Sneaky little so-and-so.

"Sure," I said. "Whatever you want is good with me."

"How 'bout Sampan?"

He did that on purpose. He knows Sampan is my favorite restaurant.

"What's going on here?" I asked, suspicious. "Did you get laid off or something?"

"No, honey," he said. "Actually, I was going to wait until I got home to ask you . . . but do you mind if I go fishing with Jim next weekend?"

"Why would I care?" I asked, wondering why such a request would warrant my favorite takeout food.

"Great! Thanks, honey," he said. "Do you just want the usual, then? Chicken teriyaki?"

"Sure. See you in a minute."

I hung up and stared at my phone, realizing that I'd left Angel at Olive Garden without so much as a "how-do-ya-do and good day." I dialed Angel's number, wondering how long it had taken her and Janice to figure out that I wasn't coming back.

"Beth? Are you okay?" Angel answered after the first ring. "You totally ditched me."

"Yeah, I'm sorry about that. I—"

"I thought us girls were supposed to stick together."

"No, you're thinking of gummy bears," I said. "Anyway, I'm sorry, okay? It's just that I—"

"I know, you ran into Charlie."

"How did you know?"

"I went looking for you and ran into him myself."

Duh.

"So, are you okay? Was it awful?" she asked.

"It wasn't that bad," I said, replaying the conversation we'd had for the millionth time.

"Really?" Angel sounded surprised. "I would have freaked out, myself. I mean it's bad enough running into your ex-boyfriend, but to run into him while he's out with the very girl he cheated with."

"WHAT?"

Silence.

"Angel?" My heart was pounding.

"Did I say something wrong? What did I do?" She sounded like a five-year-old who'd just finger-painted the living room walls.

"Please, if you would, tell me *exactly* what happened when you came looking for me."

"I, uh, well—"

"Angel."

"Well, we were sitting there for, like, twenty minutes, so I told Janice I'd better go see what was wrong, you know? Thinking maybe you'd gotten sick or something," Angel said. "So I went to the ladies' room, but you weren't in there, and I was, like, what the heck? You know? So, I was walking back when I saw him, and I just knew, right? He saw me too and kind of smiled and waved, so I went over to the table and was doing the whole 'how are you and what are you up to these days' thing when I look over at the girl he's with and it's *her*. I figured out immediately what had happened. You'd walked by, seen them, had some form of a freak-out, and left. I went back to our table and told Janice that your husband had called with an emergency, so you'd had to leave. How did you get home, by the way?"

"I caught a bus and then walked," I muttered.

"Wow," Angel said. "So, what really happened, then?"

"He stopped me on my way to the bathroom, and when I asked who he was there with, he just said a friend without even specifying a gender," I said. "Is that why he stopped me? So that I wouldn't go in the bathroom and see her? How could I have forgotten how sneaky he is? I can't believe how wound up I got—"

"You got wound up?"

"Shush it!"

"Sorry."

My face grew hot as the humiliation set in. Replaying the conversation with this new information cast it into an entirely different light. *If I ever see him again . . .*

"Beth?" Angel asked after a moment. "Are you okay?"

"Yeah, whatever," I said, deciding Charlie didn't deserve the compliment of occupying any more of my attention. "It's no big deal. I'm already over it."

"Sure?"

"Yes. Let's move on."

"Okay, are you ready to hear about the rest of my lunch?" Angel asked.

"I am, as they say, all ears."

"After you left, the first thing she launched into was this sort of financial lecture," Angel said. "Hinting that maybe I should reign in my spending a little or poor Danny would never be able to climb out of debt."

"Wow. What did you say?" I asked, congratulating myself on not dwelling on Charlie. Charlie, Charlie, Charlie. Charlie. Charlie . . .

"I just kind of humored her," Angel said. "What could I have said that would've made any difference? I mean, it was unbearable at first. But then she started talking about the downward spiral of morals today, specifically in the entertainment industry, and I realized that I actually agreed with her."

"Wow. Who knew Janice was a closet hippie?"

"Or that I was a closet conservative."

"Then the lunch was a success?"

"Now, that's a hard one to call," Angel said. "I mean, she's still Janice, after all. Just because we both think everything on television is evil doesn't mean I'm going to start singing Primary songs in her living room."

"And that's why you will always be a failure."

"Ha ha."

"Jesus wants me for a sun-*beam*," I sang. "Come on, Angel, take it away. I know you know this one."

"To shine for him each day," she sang back. "I do know that one."

"Oh, hey, I forgot to ask. When do I get my pony?"

"You don't get a pony anymore."

"What!"

"You didn't complete the assignment. I'm sorry, but the contract is now void. There will be no pony."

"But I—"

"Nope."

"With the—"

"Sorry."

"And we—"

"Not a chance."

"Can I have a goat, then?"

"On that note," Angel said, laughing, "I'm gonna go. I'll call you later."

"Yeah, yeah. Talk to you later."

While I was on the phone with Angel, I'd missed a call. But gained a voice mail message. Looking at the phone number, I was surprised to see that it was Lady's.

The minute I heard her tearful voice, I knew. Long before she said it.

Lady was pregnant.

# Chapter 12

*But Jesus said, suffer little children, and forbid them
not, to come unto me: for such is the kingdom of heaven.*

—Matthew 19:14

"LAST TIME WE MET, I gave you an assignment," Dr. Farb says. "Did
you do it?"

"Yes. I spent an entire hour on the thing," I say proudly. "It
was harder than I thought it would be to write a memory from
someone else's point of view . . . but I think I did a marvelous
job."

"Would you like to read it to me?" Dr. Farb asks.

"Should I act it out?"

Dr. Farb chuckles and shakes his head. I pull a piece of paper out
of my pocket and unfold it, clearing my throat.

"When Lady was six years old," I begin in my best impersonation of a storyteller's voice, "she came home from school one day very
upset. Whatever was bothering her remained a mystery until the next
morning, when she could no longer hold in the question she'd been
trying to answer on her own the entire night before.

"'Mommy?' Two blue eyes peeked around the doorway."

"'Yes, honey?' Mom shut off the blow-dryer and turned to her dithering daughter.

"'Mommy . . .'

"'What is it, Lady?' Mom was becoming concerned.

"'Where's my older brother? Why don't I see him anymore?'

"'What are you talking about, Lady? You don't have an—'

"Mom's heart dropped, along with the blow-dryer. Looking back at that moment, she would wonder how she'd known Lady was referring to Jesus. Regardless, it sent her on a spiritual journey that would take us from Christian born-again churches to Baptist revivals to every variation in between.

"Lady found her older brother at The Church of Jesus Christ of Latter-day Saints. Mom found her future husband. I found a really annoying kid named Greg who smelled funny and had punch-stained teeth, but that's not important.

"From then on, Mom called Lady her 'spirit child.'"

"That was very good," Dr. Farb says with an encouraging smile.

"Do you want to know my childhood nickname? Tooters. For obvious reasons. In my defense, I would like to know what baby, surviving entirely on dairy, doesn't get a little gas now and then. I spent my entire life trying to live down that nickname. Lady's spent her entire life trying to live up to hers."

As soon as I heard Lady's voice mail, I made the twenty-minute drive to her apartment in ten minutes. I was relieved when I got there to find that Chance had left for work. I wasn't up to seeing him quite yet. This being my first time comforting a pregnant, unwed older sister, I'm not sure if I said or did all the right things. I did manage to pry the giant knife from her hands, though . . . okay, maybe it was just a TV remote—but it had sharp corners.

My most notable accomplishment, however, was convincing Lady to tell Mom. She wanted to do it over the phone or with an e-mail, but I warned her that anything but a face-to-face would only make things harder. And anyway, who can resist a crying pregnant woman? Plenty of people over the phone, very few in person.

After I left, I was so engrossed in planning the best approach for breaking the news to Mom (a skit or play, perhaps?), that the sound of someone calling my name was akin to the annoyance of a buzzing bee: Something I could hear, but certainly didn't pause to pay any attention too.

"Beth. Oh, my goodness, are you deaf?"

I glanced up at the person holding my arm and jumped back in surprise.

"JoJo? What are you doing here?"

"Me?" She laughed and looked at me like I was playing a joke on her. "I live here. What are *you* doing here?"

"Right, sorry." I shook my head and chuckled. "I was just visiting Lady."

"Oh, how is she these days? I know we live in the same apartment complex and all, but I never see her."

"She's good; she's good." I fell into step beside JoJo. "But 'how are you' is a better question. I never talk to you anymore."

I left out the part where that was entirely her fault.

"Yeah, well, school and work have been crazy." JoJo paused at a flight of steps and looked uncertain for a moment. "Hey, do you want to come up for a minute? I don't think you've seen the place since before Ted and I got married."

"Sure."

"We got new couches over a month ago," she said, unlocking her door. "They're kind of showy, but you'll like them."

I followed her in and nodded my approval as I looked around. All the furniture looked new and shiny and untouched.

"I'm sorry it's such a mess," JoJo said, fluffing one of the couch cushions and wiping at some imaginary dust. "I've been running errands all day and haven't had a chance to tidy yet."

"Yeah," I said, searching for something out of place to give validity to her concerns but finding nothing. "It's a good thing Martha Stewart's not here to see this. It would break her heart."

"Whatever." JoJo laughed. "Can I get you something to drink?"

"No, I'm fine." I plopped down on one of the couches and JoJo stepped toward me with a nervous expression. "What?" I asked.

"It's nothing. It's just, um, would you mind taking off your shoes? Ted doesn't like it when, you know. That's just how his family is."

"Yeah, yeah, sorry," I said, taking off my shoes and putting them by the door. I found myself sitting down more carefully than I had before, hoping I wasn't wrinkling or squishing the cushions. I could feel my body tense up as I tried to exist in this environment without leaving any evidence of it.

"So, how have you been? How's school?" I asked as JoJo settled into the seat across from me, almost hovering above it.

"It's okay." She fidgeted with her hands. "I'm thinking of dropping out, actually."

"What? But didn't you have, like, a 3.8? And you're only a few credit-hours away from your bachelor's."

"More like a year." JoJo's fidgeting intensified. "Anyway, it takes up a lot of my time, and Ted would really like me to be home more. Besides, what will I need a bachelor's degree for when I start having kids?"

I was struck dumb for a moment, unable to respond to such a completely uncharacteristic thing for JoJo to say.

I reviewed what I knew about her in my head. Came from a family with six brothers and sisters. Lived with me for a year before I moved back in with my parents to save for my wedding. Wanted to be a social worker since she was thirteen and her best friend ran away from home to escape an abusive father. Graduated fourth in her class in high school. Regularly donated time to charities. Got into a fistfight once because a group of kids had been picking on a homeless man. Had a secret passion for Italian food. Nope, nothing in there to indicate serious flaws in reasoning capabilities.

"What if something happened and Ted couldn't work anymore?" I asked. "It would be a lot easier to get a good job with a degree. Besides, a year is not a long time, and you're not even pregnant yet. And wouldn't you be proud to tell your children that you'd accomplished that? Even if you did end up being a housewife, there's no reason you can't be an educated housewife."

. "How are you and Mike these days?" She asked in an awkward attempt to change the subject. "Are you trying for kids yet?"

"JoJo, I—"

We both turned at the sound a key in the door. The person on the other side fidgeted with the lock for a moment before throwing open the door.

"JoJo, how many times do I have to tell you to keep the door locked, even when you're home?" Ted said as he burst in. He paused when he saw me and then broke into a wide smile.

"Beth, how nice to see you! It's been too long. How's Mike?" He slipped off his shoes and came over to me, taking my hand in his and shaking it affectionately.

"He's good, we're good." I smiled, sneaking a glance at JoJo, whose eyes were glued to Ted.

"Wonderful." He released my hand and went into the kitchen, calling out. "Did you want something to drink, Beth? I'll bet JoJo forgot to even ask."

I was watching JoJo as he said this. She stared at her hands, expressionless. "Actually, she did ask, and I'm fine. Thanks, though."

"Great," he said as he came back into the living room and handed me a glass of fruit punch.

"Thanks." I took it and sipped politely. "You know, I was just about to ask JoJo when you guys would be free for dinner. It's been so long since we've all gone out together. I know Mike would love to see you again."

That was a bit of a lie. Mike didn't care one way or the other, but I was afraid if I left without more than a casual "let's get together sometime," I'd never see JoJo again.

"I was thinking the same thing," Ted said, sitting beside me and leaning in. I casually scooted farther away. "It's just that JoJo is always at one of her classes, it seems. I can never get a spare moment with her."

"That must be rough," I said with feigned sympathy. "But in a few short months, that will all be over."

Ted shot a look at JoJo, who winced. I leaned toward her automatically, causing a splash of my punch to fall onto the carpet.

"Oh, my gosh, I am so sorry," I cried, setting down my glass and jumping up. "I didn't mean to. Where's a towel? I'll clean it up."

"That's fine, Beth," Ted said through clenched teeth. "JoJo will take care of it."

JoJo jumped up and ran into the kitchen, coming back a moment later with a damp cloth and some carpet cleaner. I stepped out of her way as she kneeled down and began scrubbing.

"Well, Beth, I'm sure you've got things to do and places to be," Ted said, rising from his seat.

"Um, yeah," I said, backing toward the door. "So, what night do you guys want to come over? Mike could barbecue some steaks or something. It'll be great."

JoJo stopped scrubbing, her hand paused over the stain. Ted looked from her to me and back.

"Does Friday sound good?" I asked in one last desperate attempt.

"Friday?" he asked, his voice far away. He was staring at JoJo.

"Yeah, around seven?"

"Friday? Seven?" he repeated.

"Great, see you then." I put on my shoes and opened the door. "Mike will be so excited. See you then . . . bye, JoJo."

I closed the door behind me and leaned against it, sucking in a deep breath. I was way out of my league.

# Chapter 13

And again, verily I say unto you, if after thine enemy
has come upon thee the first time, he repent and come
unto thee praying thy forgiveness, thou shalt forgive him,
and shalt hold it no more as a testimony against thine
enemy—And so on unto the second and third time; and
as oft as thine enemy repenteth of the trespass wherewith
he has trespassed against thee, thou shalt forgive him,
until seventy times seven.

—Doctrine and Covenants 98:39–40

"SO AT THIS POINT you and Michael were getting along?" Dr. Farb
interrupts me.

"Yeah. In fact, the night I found out Lady was pregnant, I got
home and Mike was waiting for me with takeout. He was so sweet
and understanding that night, just listening to me talk about everything that was on my mind . . ."

"But that didn't last?"

"Of course not." I throw my hands up. "The very next day we
were fighting about my hair. I'd pulled it back and Mike was teasing
me—but not in a cute, funny way. It was like he was trying to tell
me he didn't like the way I looked without actually telling me that he
didn't like the way I looked."

"And this bothered you?" Dr. Farb writes something in his notebook.

"Of course it did. It got me thinking about, you know, when
I get older and have babies. I'm not always going to be pretty. I'm

*sitting here wondering if his love decreases as my butt increases. I don't want to be worried that I'll get dumped for some hot nineteen-year-old after I've given the best years of my life to him."*

*"Why is that such a specific concern for you?" Dr. Farb asks.*

*"What? I don't know." I frown and think for a moment. "I just feel so tense all the time. Like at any moment the other shoe is going to drop and everything that I've built is going to come crashing down around me. I mean, he seems so perfect, right? But nobody's that perfect, so he must be hiding something."*

*"Do you think he's hiding something?"*

*"Don't patronize me." When I say this, Dr. Farb glances up at me in surprise. "That's what I said. I mean, look at the time we saw his ex-girlfriend at the library. Something was up with that."*

*"When did this happen?" Dr. Farb turns back to his notebook and flips to a new page.*

*"A few days after I found out Lady was pregnant. We were just stopping by the library to get some books and movies and then— bam. We run into none other than Miss 'I'm-So-Perky-My-Hair-Is-Shaking' Kelly."*

I knew she was there before I saw her. Not because of my spider-sense or power of discernment. I knew she was there because Mike went perfectly still, and his cheeks turned a flaming red. He always has the same reaction when he's around an ex-girlfriend, unfortunately for him.

"MIKEY. Oh, my gosh, how are you!"

When I turned to face the owner of the voice, I expected her to be standing there in full cheerleader uniform, waving a pom-pom in my face. I wish she had been because then I could have shoved the darn thing down her throat.

"Kelly." He coughed more than said her name, glancing between us like a cornered dog.

"And who is this?" she asked, brimming with enthusiasm as she leaned toward me but keeping her eyes on Mike.

"This is Beth," I said, my voice dripping with sarcasm. "His *wife*. We've met before—at our wedding."

"Oh, that's right." She let out an obnoxious giggle. "I'm such a forgetful dope."

"And how about you?" I asked, flashing my teeth like knives. "You found that special someone yet?"

"Oh, not yet." She let out another giggle and stepped back. "Need to work on my lasso skills if I'm gonna rope one in."

I glanced at Mike, wondering how he could have dated— nay almost married—someone who murders metaphors so heartlessly.

"Well, keep looking." I patted her shoulder. "I'm sure it'll happen for you someday."

"Goodness knows I've had my share of close calls." She giggled again and punched Mike in the arm.

I imagined throwing off my coat, rolling up my sleeves, and giving her a swift left hook.

"Too bad that doesn't count for anything." Okay, that was a bit cruel, but hello? What about her last comment? If that's not a swipe at me, I don't know what is.

She giggled again but forgot to smile when she did it. There was an awkward silence where we all stared at each other.

"It was really nice seeing you, Kelly," Mike said, squeezing her shoulder.

"Thanks, Mike. You, too." She said the words softly and didn't bother to follow it with a giggle. As she began backing away, her eyes flicked over to me. She gave a weak wave and then turned and disappeared around a corner.

I counted to twenty in my head and then swung around to face Mike, my ears burning.

"What was that?" I asked in an angry whisper.

"I could ask you the same question," Mike said, throwing down the book he'd been holding and walking towards the exit.

"Where are you going?" I asked. He was walking so fast I couldn't catch up to him.

As soon as we were outside, he slowed but didn't stop.

"Mike? Where are you going? Michael, I'm talking to you."

"I'm not sure I want to talk to *you* right now, Beth," he said, pulling out the car keys and unlocking the door.

"What? I'm the one who should be mad. I'm the one—"

He slipped into the car and slammed the door, cutting me off. I stared at him in shock for a moment. He had started the car and was glaring at me through the windshield. I got in but made sure to slam the door so that he knew I was madder than he was . . . wasn't I?

We drove in silence for a moment. I was plotting the best way to attack him, debating between the wounded bird and the "I will survive" approach when he interrupted my train of thought.

"That was mean, Beth. Mean."

I opened my mouth to respond, but no words came out.

"You know I broke it off with her. You know she was crushed—and then to just go and throw the whole thing in her face like that. You have a lot of faults, Beth, but I never thought mean-spirited was one of them."

I blinked hard as angry tears escaped down my cheeks. I didn't deserve this. I most certainly did not deserve this.

"I've never been so embarrassed. I . . . I just don't even know what to say."

"Are you finished?" I asked through clenched teeth.

He didn't respond.

"So you're still in love with her, then?"

"When did I ever say I was in love with her?" Mike asked.

"You sang to her." I sniffled. "You've never sung to me."

"What?"

"That one time." I pointed my finger at him in accusation. "You told me. You guys were at that karaoke bar, and you got up and sang the theme from *Say Anything.*

"Come *on,* Beth," he yelled, slamming his fist on the steering wheel.

"Why are you so upset, then?" Tears were streaming down my face now. "Why are you rushing to poor Kelly's defense? Poor Kelly, with the broken heart. You don't even care about what she said to me."

"What? What did she say to you that was so offensive?"

"She . . . well, she . . ." For the life of me, I could not remember what she had said that made me so mad. Maybe it was the way she said it. Yeah, that was it.

"Yeah, that was it," I said.

"What?"

"I mean, it was the way she said it."

"Stop feeling sorry for yourself," Mike snapped. "You're looking for a reason to be upset."

"Excuse me? How should I feel when we run into the girl whose pictures you still keep in a box in your parent's basement?" I licked a tear off my lip. "If I still had pictures of my ex-boyfriends, you'd freak out. As it is, you get mad at me for even mentioning them."

"That's not the same thing."

"How is it not the same thing? You're allowed to be jealous about the men in my past, but I have to be the goodwill ambassador?"

"If we ran into one of your ex-boyfriends, I would at least be polite to him," Mike pointed out.

"Even if they were hitting on me in front of your face?"

He just stared straight ahead as he pulled into our driveway. He turned off the ignition but didn't move. I unbuckled my seat belt and put my hand on the door handle but stayed in the seat, wondering what I should say. The fight had gotten out of control. I was feeling like I'd done something wrong, like I should apologize. That wasn't right. *He* should apologize, not me.

"I guess I shouldn't be mad," I said, sniffing hard and wiping at my cheeks. "After all, I ran into Charlie yesterday . . ."

He gripped the steering wheel so hard his knuckles turned white. He said the word so softly that I didn't hear him at first.

"Where?" he said again.

"I was at Olive Garden with Angel." I felt a flush of satisfaction at his obvious discomfort. "He stopped me when I was heading to the bathroom."

"So you talked to him? Alone?"

"Yes."

"And?"

"And we just talked for a second." I paused, wondering if I should say it. I said it. "He said he misses me."

He gave a small nod, pulled the keys out of the ignition and walked into the house. I stared after him, wondering if I'd won the fight. And if it was worth it.

Mike and I stayed at separate ends of the apartment, with me in the bedroom glaring at the small TV on our dresser, wondering why there was nothing good enough on to distract me from the crushing weight of my self-disgust and blind hurt.

I was in the middle of a fantasy in which Mike begs for my forgiveness with a crushed and decidedly fatter Kelly watching when my cell phone rang, startling me back to reality.

"Angel, I'm not really in the mood to talk right now."

"I don't care," she whined. "I need you."

"Fine." I sighed heavily. "But I'm in a bad mood, so you can't hold anything I say against me."

"I never do." She chuckled. "What's wrong, anyway? Mike not giving it up?"

"Ha ha," I muttered. "We just had a fight."

"What about?"

"Ran into Kelly."

"Ah." She paused. "Well, that sucks, but we need to talk about me."

I laughed.

"Guess who called me today?" She asked.

"Santa Claus?"

"No. He never returns my calls," she said. "Besides, this is better—Club Sound."

"Why did Club Sound call you?"

"Because they want me to play a show on Friday," she screamed. "I gave them a demo CD a while ago and the guy just got back to me. Apparently one of their bands cancelled, and they'd been meaning to have me come in, anyway. Isn't that awesome? Isn't that way more important than your stupid fight?"

"That's great, Angel. I'm excited for you. Really," I said.

"Wait. This Friday?"

"Yeah. Why?" She sounded worried. "You are coming, aren't you?"

"It's just that . . . I had this dinner thing with JoJo and Ted."

"But you told me Mike was going fishing with Jim this weekend," Angel pointed out.

"Shoot. I forgot about that." I swore under my breath. I didn't exactly feel like going and talking it out with Mike, so I'd have to figure this one out on my own. "Okay, Angel. Let me call JoJo, and then I'll call you right back."

"No excuses," she warned before hanging up.

I was surprised that Ted answered when I called JoJo's cell phone.

"Hi, uh . . . is JoJo there?" I asked, feeling like I was in middle school all of a sudden.

"She's busy right now. Can I help you with something?" Ted's voice was cold and impersonal.

"Yeah, uh, this is Beth—"

"Oh, Beth. How are you?" He was all charm and good humor.

"Good. Uh, I was actually calling about dinner on Friday night?"

"You're not canceling, are you?" He sounded disappointed but in a very theatrical way.

"Not entirely," I said, searching for the right way to phrase my request. "When I invited you guys over, I forgot that Mike had planned a fishing trip."

"Oh, that's too bad."

"But our friend, Angel? Do you remember her? She's playing a show that night, and she would really like it if you guys came. You know, moral support? It wouldn't be too late or for too long."

"Hmm," he said. "Yeah, that might be fun. What time?"

"Great," I said. "Let me get all the details and call you back."

"Okay. Talk to you then."

When he hung up, I briefly wondered if, when I called JoJo's phone again, he'd still be the one answering it.

## Chapter 14

AFTER OUR ARGUMENT, MIKE and I avoided each other for the rest of the night. The next morning, in the few moments before I was fully awake, I leaned over and kissed his cheek. He made a sound in his sleep and smiled, wrapping his arms around me and pulling me close. Then I remembered.

Wondering what I should do, I pretended to be asleep until he awoke a few minutes later. I felt his body tense and knew he remembered too. Then he relaxed and squeezed me, kissing my ear.

"What time do you work today?" he asked, his voice still husky from sleep.

"Ten," I said, scooting as close to him as I could get.

"Okay." He kissed me again and rolled out of bed. "Let's get some breakfast, then."

Mike left for work an hour later, leaving me with an hour to kill on my own. I went outside to grab the mail and on my way saw a moving truck pull into the house across the street. A woman was standing in the front yard, guiding the vehicle in. She saw me watching her and waved. I waved back and then hesitated. Maybe I should go say "hello" and "welcome to the neighborhood" and all that. Maybe I could actually make a friend on this street.

"Hi. I'm Beth Loxstedt," I said, after I'd crossed the street and shook her hand. "Are you just moving in?"

"Oh, yes." She laughed. "Such a pain. I'm Theresa, by the way. How long have you been here?"

"Just under a year," I said. We were momentarily distracted by the moving men, who'd thrown open the truck doors and were grunting as they pulled down a heavy wood dresser.

"Be careful," she yelled at the men. "That's an antique."

"It's beautiful," I said, gesturing to the dresser.

"Better be for how much I paid for it." She laughed again. "So, is that your house? It's lovely. I like what you've done with the flower garden."

I followed her gaze and realized she thought the whole house was mine. I let out an embarrassed chuckle.

"Thank you, but that's actually not my house," I said. "My husband and I rent the little apartment attached to it."

She looked at where I was pointing and winced.

"Oh." She seemed to be struggling for something to say. "It's . . . nice . . . too."

"Thanks." I took a step back. "It's actually very cozy inside. We were lucky to have found it."

"Well, that's nice." She turned back to the moving men and began to yell and point.

I decided she would most likely continue to ignore me until I left, and I was trying hard to be insulted by her obvious snub, but the very fact that she behaved that way made it difficult for me to respect her enough to care what she thought in the first place. I swear, these people think being poor is contagious.

When I passed Theresa's house a little while later, a group of women had gathered around her, talking and laughing and pointing at her expensive furniture. She would fit in just fine. I felt a pang and admitted to myself that it hurt me that I didn't fit in, but only on a primal level.

Did people really only like each other because they looked and talked the same? Because they didn't threaten their fragile sense of reality, or challenge their quickly made but tightly held assumptions?

"Beth? Are you okay?"

I'd been so engrossed in my internal rant that I'd arrived at Barnes and Noble, gone inside, and was now glaring at the time clock.

"Hey, Jake," I said, punching in and backing out of his way. "Just getting here?"

"Yeah. And it's already going to be a long day. A customer stopped me on my way in and asked me to look up a book for her." He laughed and held up his motorcycle helmet. "I'm standing there in my jacket with my helmet in my hand, and she wants me to look up a book for her."

"Must be a regular," I said. "Did you blow her off?"

"Nah." Jake hung up his jacket and set his helmet down. "I was standing, like, two feet away from the book she wanted, so I just reached over and handed it to her."

"Well, aren't you Mr. Customer Service. I would have kicked her in the shins, myself."

"Yeah. Wouldn't you get fired for that kind of thing?"

"Not while I'm off the clock." I followed him out to the sales floor and began my assignment for the day, which was to shelve new releases in their proper sections. Exciting stuff.

"Do you work here?" a man in slacks and a golf shirt asked, interrupting my progress in the religion section.

"Yes." I said forcing a smile. "Is there something I can help you find?"

"Yeah. I'm looking for *Mormon Myths: Great Lies of the LDS Church.*"

"Follow me." I led him to a large display and held out one of the books from it.

"Have you read this?" he asked, taking the book and flipping through it.

"No, I haven't." I turned to leave.

"Are you Mormon, then? Is that why?"

"As a matter of fact, I am."

"Well, read this." He waved the book in my face. "And you won't be anymore."

Before I continue, let me recap some things, here. Older sister: pregnant. Good friend JoJo: trying desperately to cut me out of her life. Husband: thinks I'm a mean jerk. Neighbors: snobby. This guy: not in the mood for.

"Really?" I said with mock enthusiasm. "Because, you know, my faith is *so* fragile that this one single book will completely wipe out the years of dedication, blessings, and spiritual experiences I've had as a Mormon. I am so weak-minded that some man whom I've never met and know nothing about will, with his closed-minded and overused tactics, be able to shake me free of my faith so that I may frolic about in sin without the guilt of knowing that my actions mean anything. Please, kind sir, free me of my morals."

"Wow." He backed away. "I didn't mean anything by it."

"No, wait. I'm sorry," I said, holding my hand to my forehead. "I'm sure the book is very wonderful and insightful."

He looked down at the book and put it back on the shelf. "If you need someone to make your day go better . . ."

"Beth, call 206. Beth, 206," Jake said into the store intercom.

He winked at me, and I shook my head, trying not to gag. "I've got to get back to work. Enjoy your book."

I picked the book back up off the shelf and gave it to him, and then walked over to the nearest store phone and dialed extension 206.

"What's up?" I asked when Jake answered.

"Yeah, some guy named Charlie is here to see you. He's at the customer service desk."

My heart dropped, and I considered making a run for it.

# Chapter 15

*Thou tellest my wanderings: put thou my tears*
*into thy bottle: are they not in thy book?*

—Psalm 56: 8

"LET'S TALK ABOUT STAN *a little," Dr. Farb suggests. "You've hardly*
*mentioned him at all."*

*I grunt and lean back in my chair, staring up at the ceiling. I try*
*to imagine little faces in the uneven white paint.*

*"I can count on one hand the number of times I've seen my*
*father since he left when I was four." Staring at the ceiling instead*
*of Dr. Farb makes me feel like I'm talking to myself, so I continue to*
*stare upward.*

*"The most vivid memory was when I was five, and he took Lady*
*and me to Great America. Lady doesn't believe I remember it but I do." I*
*pause and frown as the memory unfolds in my mind. "I remember every-*
*thing. How his head seemed to touch the tip of the sky, how he smelled like*
*coffee and cigarettes. How he never looked at me.*

*"That was the day he bought me a purple button-up shirt with*
*black triangles on it—a souvenir. It was all I had of him and I*
*treasured it."*

*I look back at Dr. Farb and then down at my feet. Dr. Farb watches me patiently.*

"Until I was twelve," *I continue.* "Mom was helping me clean out my closet and when she found it, she asked what it was, as it was obviously not something I could fit into anymore. I gazed at it sadly and explained that it was from Stan. From the day he took us to Great America. She made a weird sound and turned back to the pile she was sorting through. I watched her for a moment, confused.

"'What's wrong, Mom?' I remember asking, 'Are you mad that I've kept it for so long?'

"'No, honey. No.' She looked like she wanted to say more but didn't.

"I looked at the shirt and then at her, 'What is it? What aren't you saying?'

"'It's no big deal, Betsy Boo,' she said as she stroked my arm, 'but I bought that for you.'

"I looked back at the shirt, wondering how I'd remembered it wrong.

"'When Stan took you girls there, he spent all his extra cash on his girlfriend's kids,' she continued. 'I was so mad when I met up with him. He was standing there with this big bag of toys, and you and Lady were completely empty-handed. It broke my heart. So I gave him twenty dollars and told him to go into the gift shop by the entrance and pick something out for both of you.'

"'Oh.'

"'It's not that he didn't love you,' she said, already regretting her honesty. 'He just doesn't know how to show it. It was never that he didn't love you.'

"'Right.'

"'Beth? Honey?'

"'Hey, are we going to the store later? Because I ate the last of the Oreos last night. We need more peanut butter, too.'

"'Okay, let's make a list when we finish up here.'

"Mom understood. She never brought up Great America again. When I threw the shirt away later that night, all I felt was humiliation. Humiliation that I'd held on so long to a memory that wasn't* *even real. Humiliation for imagining that our shared moment had meant as much to him as it had to me. At twelve, I realized something it takes most people a lifetime to learn. Love is not distributed evenly—if it's distributed at all."*

"What are you doing here?"

"It's nice to see you, too." Charlie laughed, pulling me into a hug before I knew what he was up to.

Jake watched the scene unfold with an amused smile, and I shot him a dirty look before grabbing Charlie's arm and leading him away. I stopped when I reached some chairs in a far corner of the store and gestured for him to sit while I plopped down across from him.

"How are you? You look great," Charlie said, leaning toward me.

"Hmm," I muttered, my expression suspicious.

"How's the old gang? You still hanging out with JoJo and Angel?"

"It's only been two years," I pointed out.

"I know, I know." He held up his hands in defense. "Is Angel a famous singer yet?"

"Not yet, but she's playing a show on Friday," I said. "We're all pretty excited about that."

"Hey, that's great," he said. "Where at?"

"It's called Club Sound. I've never been there, but Angel said it's very classy."

"That's great," he said, resting his elbows on his knees and his chin in his hands. "Maybe I should go? I could finally meet your mysterious husband. We might even hit it off, become friends."

"Stop it," I snapped. "Do you even care that I'm married? Or is this just some kind of game for you?"

"I care." He became serious and leaned back, staring at me. "I care."

"How's Scarlet?"

He winced and looked away.

"That was a rotten thing to do," I said.

"What was?"

"You know what I'm talking about." I could feel my ears begin to burn. "You should have told me."

"It was the first time I'd seen you." He leaned toward me and reached for my hand. I pulled away. "I didn't want our first conversation in over two years to be about that."

"Why not? Our last one was."

"Beth . . ." He let out a frustrated sigh and put his head in his hands. "What I did—it was just stupid. I'm not pretending it wasn't the biggest mistake of my life."

"That's funny," I said. "Most people don't take the biggest mistakes of their lives out to lunch."

"Stop it," he said, looking hurt. "I'm sorry I didn't tell you, okay? It's not what you think it is, anyway. Scarlet and I are just friends. But if you want me to . . . I'll leave you alone; if you want me to."

We fell into silence. I was ashamed to admit that I didn't want him to leave me alone. What was I thinking? What was I hoping was going to happen here? Did I want him to rescue me from my perfect husband? My perfect life? This man—who'd cheated and lied and then run away like a coward . . . I was betraying Mike more every second that I sat here.

"I have to get back to work," I said, standing up on shaking legs.

"Beth." He grabbed my hand. "If I could have done it over . . ."

"I'm glad things happened the way they did," I lied.

He stood and pulled me to him. "I'm not asking you to leave him. Just look at your life and see if you're really happy. If, maybe, you could be happier . . ."

I pushed him away hard. "You're the cheater. Don't turn me into one."

"Beth—"

"Listen, Charlie, I know you've always loved a challenge," I said, backing away. "And I must look like a pretty good one right now, but this isn't a game. This is my life. If you care about me as much as you say you do, you'll leave me alone."

I turned and walked away, congratulating myself on what I thought was a pretty good exit line.

# Chapter 16

After my visit with Charlie, my day only got worse. The anti-Mormon guy I'd gone off on earlier complained to my manager (even though I had apologized), two of my coworkers called in sick, a man who smelled of cheese and vegetables spent an hour following me around the store, and a girl came in demanding a book for school, the title of which she couldn't remember, but she did know it was something like *The* 'something' 'something'.

I decided that, since this was shaping up to be a pretty rotten day, I might as well drag Lady over to Mom's and get that whole thing over with. Really go out in style.

"Beth," Lady said, when I showed up at her apartment unannounced. "You said we'd do this when I was ready . . ."

"Change of plans." I grabbed her purse and ushered her out the door. "*I'm* ready and that's good enough."

"Beth . . . Beth." Lady trailed behind me, dragging her feet. "What are we going to say? Oh no, I think I'm gonna throw up."

She stopped and leaned over some bushes, taking deep breaths.

"Are you okay?" I turned back, concerned.

"Yeah, yeah. False alarm."

"Okay," I said, grabbing her purse and digging through it. "But if you're feeling sick, we're taking your car."

By the time we pulled up to the house, Lady was stone-faced and ready for battle. I wasn't as worried as she was, considering Mom had already dealt with the blow of Lady moving in with her boyfriend. This was the next logical step on the road of disappointments, and I didn't think she'd be too surprised.

That's when Mom's the scariest—when someone comes out of left field with something she's not expecting. Like getting suspended from school for attacking a hall monitor. (By the way, since when is flipping a person off considered an attack?)

When we walked in, Rory and Jeri were watching TV in the living room. Mom was in the kitchen having a heated conversation over the phone.

"I don't care," Mom snapped. "This is unacceptable. Frankly, I'm very disappointed."

She smiled at us when we walked in and held up a finger.

"Uh-huh . . . uh-huh . . . okay, but I've got company, so I need to go," she said. "I want you to think about what you've done. I'll give you a call later so we can talk about this more."

"Who was that?" I asked when she'd hung up.

"The bank," she answered. "They made an error and bounced my account. They say they'll put all the money back in, but that doesn't change the fact that all these people I wrote checks to now think I can't manage my money."

"That sucks," I offered.

"Just part of being a grown-up, so get used to it," Mom said. "What are you guys doing here? Come to take your favorite mother to a movie?"

I cleared my throat awkwardly. "I . . . uh, we came over because Lady and I need to . . . actually, just Lady . . . uh—"

"I'm pregnant," Lady said, bursting into tears.

"Way to ease into it," I muttered.

The television went quiet, and I turned to see Rory and Jeri standing in front of it, staring at us in shock.

"Rory, Jeri—go play outside," Mom snapped.

"Mom," Rory complained. "We're not five."

"Well, you won't make it to fifteen if you don't do what I say," Mom said. "Go. Now."

We stood in silence until the door closed behind them. Then Mom looked at me as if I had bad news, too.

"Let me guess—you're getting a divorce," she muttered.

"Not yet." I chuckled nervously, pulling out a chair from the table and sitting in it. Lady sat down beside me and we both stared up at Mom silently.

"You're sure?" Mom asked.

"Yes." Lady's voice was barely a whisper.

"And it's Chance's?" Mom was pacing in front of us.

"Mom!" Lady said, offended.

"Oh, don't you dare 'Mom' me." Mom stopped pacing and faced Lady. "You spit on everything I've taught you, everything I've raised you to be, and you have the nerve to get defensive? Do you even know what it means to have a baby? How selfish it is to get pregnant when you have no family and no way to provide for it?"

I could feel Lady shaking beside me so I jumped in. "Mom, I'm sure Lady—"

"Shut up, Bethany." Mom turned her angry gaze on me. "You're not the hero here, so stop trying to fix everything."

I clamped my mouth shut and blinked back tears.

"Why, Lady?" Mom fell into the chair across from us, putting her head in her hands. "How could you do this? Are you dead set on repeating all of my mistakes?"

Lady and I looked at each other, confused, and then turned back to Mom.

"What? You never—" Lady began.

"There's something I never told you two." She looked defeated. "About your father . . . about Stan and me. But you have to understand—I wasn't raised with the same kinds of values . . . or religion."

She turned to stare out the window. We waited, holding our breaths.

"I moved in with him before we got married. In my world at that time, that was just how you did things." She turned her eyes to Lady. "I got pregnant with you. He didn't want to marry me, but I made him. I didn't want to give you up, but I didn't want to raise you on my own, either."

We stared at her in shock, and I had a feeling that Lady was off the hook for this latest blunder.

"Stan did a lot of drugs. And he cheated on me. But I bore it, because I didn't want to be alone." Mom sucked in a deep breath and stared at her hands. "But one day I left him to watch you, Beth—you were only a few months old, so the day care would only take Lady. When I got home, he was stoned out of his mind, and you were screaming in your crib. He hadn't changed your diaper or fed you for six hours. I wasn't even strong enough to leave him then, but I wanted to. I don't think I ever forgave myself."

My mind was reeling. I remembered being a little girl and feeling like Mom was always mad at me. Like I was a burden. Like I was guilty of the unforgivable sin of simply being alive and needing her. I'd forgotten most of these things because after we joined the Church, she changed. Mom wasn't scared and angry anymore. She met my stepdad. She started over. But here we were, a daily reminder of all that she'd done wrong. And now she was watching Lady make all the same mistakes.

"Beth." Mom interrupted my thoughts. "Why don't you join your sisters outside. I'd like to talk to Lady alone."

"But, Mom—"

"Bethany Jane Wright." She pointed toward the back door.

"It's Loxstedt, now," I muttered under my breath as I retreated to the backyard.

"What's going on in there?" Rory ran up the second she spotted me. "Lady's gonna get it, isn't she? What did Mom say? Is it true? Lady's gonna get it."

"I left my book in there," Jeri complained, looking at me as if I could do anything about it.

"Is Lady getting it?" Rory asked.

"Enough, you little sadist." I laughed, pushing past her and plopping down on the grass. I stared up at the clouds, feeling like a teenager again. Was this the same patch of sky I used to stare at when I would come out here after a bad day at school?

I heard Jeri and Rory sit down on either side of me, a soft plucking sound to my right indicating that Rory was picking at the grass. We sat there in silence until I let out a heavy sigh to let them know they could start asking me questions again.

"Beth?" Jeri asked. "What's going on? Really?"

"Lady's preggers." I reached over and patted her knee. "Have you had 'the talk' yet?"

Jeri snickered. "Yes. Forever ago."

"Good," I said. "I'm not sure I was up to giving it to you."

"What's she going to do with it?" Rory asked quietly.

"Sell it, probably," I told her. "You can get a lot of money for a healthy baby these days."

Jeri drew back in horror, but Rory just rolled her eyes.

"She's kidding," Rory told Jeri, who relaxed. Rory stared at the house for a moment, running her hands through the pile of grass she'd created. "Does kind of make your problems seem small, though. Doesn't it?"

"Yeah," Jeri said.

"Yeah," I said.

Lady didn't say a word to me for the duration of the drive back to her apartment. I had decided that this was one of those times when cracking jokes or talking about myself might be considered inappropriate. With those two options denied me, I found myself unable to say anything to break the silence.

I pulled into a parking spot and turned off the car, waiting for her to make the next move. I could hear her sniffling, but I was afraid to turn and face her.

"I hate her," Lady said softly.

"What?" I asked, surprised. "Who? Mom?"

"She said I couldn't keep the baby."

"What? But, it's not her choice to make." I thought for a moment. "Are you sure that's what she said?"

She sniffled and stared out the window. Then shrugged and looked at me, defeated. "She gave me an ultimatum."

"Uh-huh."

"I have three choices, as far as she's concerned." Lady turned at the sound of laughter and watched two children chase each other across the parking lot. "I can give up the baby for adoption, I can marry Chance, or I can keep the baby, but have nothing to do with Mom and Dad anymore."

I sat for a moment, trying to process her choices. "At least abortion isn't one of them."

"Just because she thought we were such a mistake," Lady was talking more to herself. "Just because she regretted getting stuck with us doesn't mean I will."

"Which one are you going to do?"

"I know which one I'm *not* going to do." Lady looked down at her stomach and put both of her hands on it, the tiniest trace of a smile dancing on her lips. "I'm not giving it up. I already love it so much. I could never give it up."

# Chapter 17

*Your testimony of Jesus Christ is the most important*
*anchor that you can have to help hold you, steadfast*
*and immovable, to principles of righteousness.*

—M. Russell Ballard, "Steadfast in Christ," *Ensign*,
December 1993, 50

"I DON'T KNOW WHY *Lady and I turned out so different. I sometimes*
*wonder if the reason I made all the 'right' choices was just because*
*I was scared that if I did anything wrong, Mom would stop loving*
*me.*"

"*Is that what you believe?*" *Dr. Farb asks.*

"*No. Not really.*" *I shrug.* "*I don't think it's that simple. It's just,*
*to me, it was plain logic. You know? I mean, partying and doing*
*whatever you want seems like fun, but you always end up paying for*
*it later. Why waste my time doing something I already knew would*
*end badly?*"

*I twirl a strand of hair around my finger and think for a*
*moment.*

"*I had this friend in high school who was an atheist.*" *I chuckle*
*at the memory.* "*She was one of the smartest girls I'd ever met—but*
*so angry.*

"*One time we got into kind of a heated debate about how she thought I was spending so much of my life trying to live up to the standards of my church. I remember saying to her, 'Here's how I see it: if there's no God, then I've led a pretty clean and happy life and I'm no worse off for it. But if there is a God and I had denied him, then there would be hell to pay—literally.' She just laughed and said that was the best argument she'd heard so far, but it got me thinking . . . do I really believe in God or am I just trying to play it safe, like I always do?"*

*"Have you answered this question yet?" Dr. Farb watches me intently.*

*"Yes." I nod firmly. "And no. There are times when I feel it. When I know there's something beyond me in my life. Like this burning in my chest when I hear Angel sing . . . you can't tell me there's no God when I feel like that. But then there are long periods of time where there's nothing. It's just me in the world, alone." I feel tears stinging the back of my eyes. "Lady always was the spiritual one. She listens to her heart more than anyone I know. But I kind of think that's why she's had so much trouble in her life. The heart can be misleading. It can be impatient. She, at times, has had a stronger testimony of the Church than anyone I've ever met. And then she'll do a 180 and say it's all a cult trying to tell us how to live."*

*Dr. Farb looks at me with an understanding that makes me short of breath, but I continue without pause.*

*"To me, it's a logical choice. I've never felt it like Lady's felt it. And yes, I'm jealous of that. But I've never had to fight for it like she's had to, either. One of these days, she'll come back to it, and she'll be this amazing, inspiring woman with all these stories of what she's been through and the life she's lived . . . and I'll still be Beth. Just doing what I'm supposed to do, going through the motions."*

*"So you feel like you're missing out?" Dr. Farb asks.*

*"I guess. But it's just so much harder the way she does it . . . feeling things."*

# Chapter 18

"How will I live without you? I want to know. How will I live without you—if you ever go," I sang into my showerhead, closing my eyes and holding each note as long as I could. "How will I ever . . . ever survive—"

"Beth?" Mike knocked on the bathroom door and carefully opened it. "Are you singing?"

"Uh, no. That was the radio." I peeked out of the shower, wiping water off my face.

He chuckled and shook his head.

"It was the radio," I tried again. "It's a new station. A karaoke station."

"Baby, you don't have to lie. I think it's cute when you sing."

"Really?" I flirted. "In that case, maybe I should try a little opera."

"Have you seen my travel toothbrush?" he asked, pulling everything out of the medicine cabinet. "And there was a little hotel soap I had. A little hotel soap. Have you seen that?"

It was Friday, and Mike was rushing around the apartment at the last minute as usual, trying to pack for his fishing trip with Jim. I'd tried in vain to get him to postpone it so he could come to Angel's show at Club Sound, but apparently the allure of her music did not call as strongly to him as it did to me.

"Aw, it doesn't matter," I said, turning off the shower and grabbing my towel. "You'll smell like fish—soap or no soap."

"Sorry I can't go to Angel's show tonight," he said, wrapping his arms around me. "But I'm sure you'll be having too much fun to even notice I'm gone."

"Yeah. You're probably right. I bet there'll be lots of drummers there. You know how I love drummers."

Mike pulled his cell phone out of his pocket and began dialing a number.

"Who you calling?" I asked.

"Jim." He held the phone up to his ear. "I'm canceling the trip so I can keep an eye on you."

"Don't," I said, laughing and grabbing the phone out of his hand. "I'm just kidding. And besides, I've got Angel and Danny there to keep an eye on me. If I even think of stepping out of line, they'll tie me to a chair and administer a blessing or something."

"I love you." Mike pulled me close and kissed me. I melted into his arms, flashing back to the days when kissing like this was forbidden fruit to us and therefore a regular pastime. One of the first things to go after the wedding day is make-out sessions. Sigh.

He pulled away and kissed the tip of my nose. Then he gathered the pile of toiletries he'd created on the counter and shoved it into his bag.

"I've got to get going." Mike glanced at his watch. "Jim's waiting. I'll call you when we get to the cabin."

I followed him to the door, still wearing the towel. "Mike . . . behave yourself, okay?"

"Of course I will, babe." He threw his bag over his shoulder and picked up his fishing pole.

"Seriously. Jim's got some bad habits I don't want you picking up." I struck a seductive pose. "Just remember what you've got waiting at home."

"How could I forget?" he asked, giving me another kiss.

"Smooth. Very smooth. Now, get out of here."

"I'm not running that late," he said, glancing past me toward the bedroom.

"Go," I said, pushing him out the door.

"Bored. Bored, bored, bored," I said into my phone. "Angel— please call me. I'm bored. Bored, I say."

I hung up the phone and stared at it, chastising Angel in my head for not being at my beck and call. I picked up the remote and flipped through the channels, trying to decide between a reality show about makeovers, a reality show about home makeovers, or a *Friends* rerun. Choices, choices.

When my phone rang, I picked it up so fast that I was out of breath when I answered it.

"Did you just wake up?" Angel asked.

"No, I'm just so excited to talk to you I can't catch my breath."

"Yeah, I get that reaction a lot." She laughed. "What's up? I hear you're bored."

"Yes," I burst out. "What are you doing? If I'm left to my own devices any longer, I'll make a fort out of my couch cushions or buy a puppy or something."

"I'm not sure that my option is any better than those two," she said. "Danny and I are going over to his parents'. There's a barbecue going on, I guess."

"Hmm." I considered. "How many people will be there?"

"I dunno." She paused. "At least his whole family. Probably some neighborhood friends; I don't know."

"Do you think they'd care if I came?"

"No more than they care that I'm coming."

"Wahoo," I said. "Come get me."

"Go get yourself," she said. "I'm not driving all the way up there. Meet us at the Snows.'"

"No," I wailed. "I can't show up on my own. This is the social event of the season and I don't have a date. What will people think?"

"You poor thing. Do you remember where they live?"

"Yes." I tried to squeeze as much pouting as I could in the one word.

"Good," Angel said, oblivious to my dissatisfaction with the arrangement. "We're leaving right now, so call me when you get there."

I just made a farting sound with my mouth and hung up.

Twenty minutes later, I pulled up to the Snows' house. Before I could dial Angel's number (which was number two on my phone, so I'm not really sure if that counts as dialing) she was at my car, practically dragging me out of it.

"Angel—not in front of the neighbors," I said, as she grabbed my arm and led me up the yard to the front door.

"I'm so glad you're here," she breathed. "I'm getting crucified in there. Need a little backup."

"But I didn't bring any backup," I said, worried.

"You are the backup."

"Oh." I nodded. "That's sad. What's going on in there?"

We stopped on the porch, and Angel leaned against the door, sighing. "It's about my show, tonight. They're concerned that their precious Danny will be exposed to the seedy underbelly of society with his harlot wife leading the fray."

"There's a fray?"

"And I'm leading it."

I laughed as she opened the door and led me inside. A group of people were gathered around the kitchen counter, helping themselves to the assortment of food lined up along it. I noticed there were only three hot dogs left, so I ungraciously pushed myself into the crowd to snag one.

"Beth. How nice to see you," Janice gushed, hugging me so

hard I almost dropped my plate. "How are you and Mike? Everything okay?"

I looked at her, confused; then I remembered that the last time she'd seen me, I'd mysteriously disappeared with some sort of family emergency.

"Yes. Yes, we are great. Thank you for asking." I turned back to my plate as politely as I could, and she wandered off a moment later. I gave myself three out of a possible ten on the small talk scale.

"No, I'm going to do what my dad did," Taylor, Danny's younger brother, was saying to some other guy I didn't recognize. "I'm going to marry her young so I can train her."

"Are you serious?" the guy asked. "I could never be a complete enough person that I could make someone else what I wanted."

Angel was standing beside me and saw my confusion, so she leaned over and whispered in my ear. "It's a big joke in this family that Danny's dad married their mom when she was nineteen so he could train her. He's really proud of the fact that he did such a good job."

"What?" I asked, incredulous. I thought back to when I was nineteen, unable to imagine someone attempting to mold me at that time in my life. They'd need to have snagged me at about ten to have had any luck in that department.

"It's not like Taylor makes it sound," Janice jumped in.

"Then how is it?" Angel asked. "Because it *sounds* like us women need to be kept in line and saved from ourselves in case we start thinking too much."

"A good wife listens to her husband," Janice said pointedly.

"And a good husband listens to his wife," Angel snapped.

I shoved the hot dog in my mouth in case Angel glanced over, expecting me to jump in.

"Well, hopefully he doesn't listen if she's manipulating him," Janice said.

"If that's what you call a woman who's strong enough to stand up for herself," Angel shot back.

I looked around to see if Danny was nearby and available

to hold one of them back if it should come to fisticuffs. I could see him in the backyard talking to his father, Phil. Both were oblivious to the fight going on between the two most important women in Danny's life.

"You both have good points," Nameless Guy said. "A marriage should be equal—both sides listening to each other and making compromises when necessary."

Who was this guy?

"That's exactly what I'm trying to say, Bill," Angel said. Aha. The guy's name was Bill.

"You're too young to know how hard marriage is," Janice said, crossing her arms. "I'm glad I was lucky enough to have someone like Phil to guide me."

"How weak do you have to be to let someone else tell you who you are?" Angel asked. I sucked in a breath. She'd gone too far with that one.

"Someone else? Like, maybe . . . Jesus?" Janice asked.

"If Phil is Jesus, then I'm Satan." Angel slammed her hand down on the counter.

There was an awkward silence, and I turned to see that Phil and Danny had just walked up and were staring at Angel with shocked expressions.

"Wow, these hot dogs are really good," I said. "But boy do I have to pee . . ."

Silence.

"Angel?" I asked, grabbing her arm and hedging toward the door. "Gee, it's getting late. We better go get ready for that show tonight. You know how Satan's minions hate to be kept waiting."

# Chapter 19

*A man that hath friends must shew himself friendly:*
*and there is a friend that sticketh closer than a brother.*

—Proverbs 18:24

"THE SUMMER BEFORE *I started high school, Lady took me to a battle-of-the-bands competition. That was the first time I saw Angel."* I laugh, gesturing with my hands as I speak. *"She was belting out a No Doubt song, and I thought it was the coolest thing I'd ever seen. She looked so powerful, so ready to take over the world."*

*Dr. Farb nods for me to continue.*

*"The next year, when fate put us in the same P.E. class, I sought her out, omitting the real reason I'd insisted she be my tennis part-ner. We became best friends fast, but where she was confident and full of life, I was self-conscious and afraid. I still remember one of our most famous conversations. I'd been feeling sorry for myself because Cody Redfield had asked Sheila Black to the prom, even though I'd invested some very serious flirting time in him.*

*"I remember saying: 'I'm ugly and stupid, and I will never have a boyfriend. I will die an old maid with thirty cats.'*

"'Are you really this upset?' Angel asked me. 'Just because one stupid boy doesn't like you?'

"'Yes,' I insisted. 'I am crappy. Crappy-craparoo.'

"'You can't be,' she said firmly, 'Because I like you and I'm Angel Barlow.'

"This was a good point.

"After that, whenever I felt self-conscious, she'd always get me laughing by insisting that if she liked me, I must be cool. A lot of kids in our school were offended by Angel's unflappable self-confidence. They thought she was self-centered and narcissistic, or at the very least, faking it. I never paid attention to them, because, even if they were right, I didn't care. In a lot of ways, I think that confidence saved me."

"How so?" Dr. Farb asks.

"Do you remember how rough high school was? She was the first person—in my life, really—who made me feel like I was worth liking. Not because I cleaned the house or said funny things but just because I was me. It was a whole new way of looking at myself."

"Whatcha working on?" I asked Danny, sliding a chair up to the table next to him. He'd been hunched over a napkin with a pen ever since Angel had excused herself to Club Sound's ladies' room to warm up her voice.

"It's a letter," he said, smiling at me briefly before returning to the napkin.

I wondered how anyone could concentrate on anything with the music pounding against their ears and the dim lights flashing with the beat, but Danny was determined. I glanced around the club, hoping the crowd would get bigger by the time Angel went on. Club Sound consisted of a few small rooms underneath a print shop, all musty and smelling of sweat, but with that rundown edge that makes club-goers feel like they are hard-core without being in danger of having to prove it.

"You do realize that doesn't answer my question," I pointed out.

"It's a letter to my family." He set the pen down and sighed. "Asking them to be more accepting of Angel."

I glanced at the napkin with interest. "Why? Because of the barbecue incident?"

"It's more than that," he said. "I know Angel's not perfect. But there's so much to her—about her—that they're missing out on because they won't stop and look. Even if they completely disagree, they need to respect my choice. Angel is who I married and by rejecting her, they're rejecting me."

"Wow," I said. "Did you put all that in there?"

"I don't know." He laughed and picked up the napkin. "I'm working on it."

"Well, good luck." I patted him on the back. "It is a worthy goal."

"Isn't that your friend JoJo?" he asked, looking at the door-way.

"Finally." I jumped up and turned. "She's almost half an hour late. Any longer and they might have missed Angel's per-formance."

When I approached her, I noticed immediately that she looked windblown and frazzled . . . as if she'd chased Toto into the house before it had blown away. When she saw me, she gave me a weak smile, fidgeting with her hair.

"JoJo. I'm so glad you came." I gave her a hug, but lightly, afraid to break her. "Is everything okay? You look a little . . . frazzled."

"Yeah, I'm fine." Her voice was shaky. "Ted got a little lost on the way here."

"Where is he?" I asked, glancing past her.

"He's trying to find a parking spot."

"JoJo." I held her by the shoulders and made her look me in the eye. "What's going on?"

"What do you mean?"

"Are you honestly trying to con me right now?"

She sighed and glanced down. "Okay, but it will probably sound worse than it is . . ."

"Okay." I led us to a nearby table so we could sit down.

"Uh, well . . . when we were driving here, there was this guy in front of us," she said, picking at loose strings on her shirt. "He kept slamming on his brakes and driving real slow, so Ted started to get mad. He honked at the guy a couple times, but the guy just kept slamming on his brakes and driving real slow."

"Uh-huh."

"Well, to me, it looked like he was kind of old, so I said this to Ted, but he didn't care. Said the guy was doing it on purpose to provoke him." She stopped talking and stared at the doorway for a moment.

"Don't worry," I said, reading her mind. "I'll tell you when Ted walks in. And he'll never know you told me this, okay?"

She nodded and turned back to the loose string on her shirt. "Anyway, Ted pulls onto the shoulder and passes this guy, and I look over and see that he really was pretty old. When Ted gets in front of the guy, *he* starts slamming on his brakes and going real slow—only worse. I could tell the old guy was getting scared, so I kept begging Ted to stop, but he was saying how he needed to teach this guy a lesson—a driving lesson."

She stopped, so I put my hand over hers to stop it from fidgeting and nodded for her to continue.

"The old guy pulled over, probably to put some distance between us and him, but then Ted pulls over too and gets out of the car." She breathed in deeply and shut her eyes. "He goes over to the other guy's car and starts punching the car and hitting it and screaming at the guy. I could see that the old guy was crying and waving his arms for Ted to stop, but Ted was oblivious . . . he was just in this blind rage. I got out and tried to pull him away, but he threw me off. So I just sat there in the middle of the road, crying like a helpless idiot."

"What did he do after that?" I asked in shock. "Did he hurt the old guy?"

"No." She gave me a sad smile. "He calmed down after a minute, and then it was like nothing happened."

"What do you mean, it was like nothing happened?"

"I mean it was like nothing happened," she repeated. "I tried to talk to him about it on the way here, but he acted like he didn't even know what I was talking about."

"You're kidding," I breathed. "Has he ever done anything like this before?"

JoJo shrugged.

"JoJo," I said. "Tell me."

"A few other times," she admitted. "But never this bad, I swear."

"What else does he do?" I asked, my voice barely above a whisper.

"Beth," she pleaded. "It's really not as bad as it sounds."

I was about to press her further, but Ted walked in and immediately spotted us.

"Beth," he boomed, walking over. "There you are. We had a bit of trouble finding this place."

He laughed and shook my hand, pulling up a seat in between JoJo and me. I forced a smile and a nod, and then turned away.

"JoJo," he said, his eyes flashing. "Your hair is a mess. That's why I always tell you not to drive with the window down. Why don't you go fix it?"

She nodded and stood. "Do you know where the bathrooms are?"

"Yeah, just around that corner." I pointed and stood. "I'll go with you."

"No, she's fine," Ted said, grabbing my arm and pulling me back into my seat. "You girls and your bathroom visits. Can't do anything alone, can you?"

He laughed as JoJo hurried off.

"You know," he said, leaning close to me. "I feel like I can be honest with you, Beth."

"Really?" I asked, scooting away.

"JoJo and I have been having a few problems lately." He looked down. "I'm really worried about her, actually. Maybe you can help since you know her so well."

"Okay . . ."

"She's been getting really jealous, you know?" He put his hand over mine. "Thinking that I'm cheating on her and things like that. She freaks out and accuses me of all these crazy things. And . . . and—"

"What?" I asked, putting my hand on his back as a way to pull it out of his.

"She hits me," he said the words softly, as if it hurt him to admit it.

Did he really think I was buying this? This big, strong man falling victim to a small, shaken shell of the girl I used to know?

"Well, do you do anything to provoke her?" I asked.

He opened his mouth to answer just as JoJo and Angel walked up.

"Ten minutes till show time," Angel squealed. "Where's Danny boy?"

"He's over there," I said, gesturing to a table in the corner. "Are you nervous?"

"Are you kidding?" Angel struck a pose, making JoJo giggle. "They're gonna love me."

"It's not hard to see why," Ted said, winking at Angel and grabbing her arm.

"Excuse me?" Angel asked, drawing back.

"It was just a joke," Ted said.

"And some jokes are inappropriate," I snapped before I could stop myself.

He looked at me. "I'm not the one wearing the tight shirt here."

"Oh, that is it." Angel threw up her arms and stormed off.

"What's her problem?" Ted asked, looking at me like I should be as confused as he was.

"Are you serious?" I asked. "Do you really think this good guy act is working on us?"

The words flew out before I could stop myself.

"What do you mean?" His voice was frosty.

"I mean you are a jerk, and everyone knows it." I stood. "The only reason we put up with you is so we can see JoJo. When you let her out of her cage."

He stood up so fast that his chair fell back. "I can see that JoJo has some bad influences in her life. That she needs to get rid of."

"Yeah. You."

His face turned red, and his fist was clenched. I took a step back but held his gaze.

"I don't need to put up with this kind of treatment." He turned to JoJo. "I'll be out in the car."

She watched him walk off with a stricken expression.

"JoJo." I walked toward her, my arms out. "I'm so sorry. I just—"

"Leave me alone, Beth." When she turned to me, her eyes were blazing. "I can't believe you just humiliated my husband like that. If you cared about me at all, you would have just kept your stupid mouth shut."

"What?"

"You think you're helping?" she asked. "You think you're just going to rush in and make everything all better? You don't know one thing about my life."

I opened my mouth, but no words came out.

She stared at me for another moment; then turned and left. I stared after her, still unable to speak.

I had the feeling that, in my anger, I'd only made things worse. And, in so doing, just seen the last of JoJo.

# Chapter 20

"BETH? ARE YOU OKAY?" Angel asked, sitting at the table I had been using as a shelf for my forehead.

After JoJo had left, I'd rested my head on the table and stared at the grimy floor beneath my feet, replaying the conversation, trying to figure out what I should have done differently.

"No," I muttered, without moving.

"Stop pouting," she said. "You were just standing up for a friend. Anyone would have done it."

"JoJo's right," I said, looking at Angel with a sour expression. "I don't know anything about her life. Who am I to get right in there and say what I think? Half the time, I'm not even sure what I think."

"Seriously, Beth." Angel rubbed my back. "I'm proud of you. Not a lot of people would have stood up to someone like that."

"But I only made things worse."

"Worse than if you'd stayed silent?" Angel asked. "At least

now JoJo knows that when she's ready to face whatever's going on with her and Ted, she's got you in her corner. Right?"

"Yeah."

"You okay?" Angel asked again.

I nodded.

"Good." She smiled. "Because it's time to focus on me. I'm going on in a few minutes, and I need to know that you will be giving me your full and raptured attention."

"Uh, I do notta thinka that means what you thinka that means." I laughed.

"Yes, it does," she said. "I'm gonna go set up. Go keep an eye on Danny for me. I don't want him to become so overwhelmed by the evil in here that he decides to get a tattoo or become a liberal or something."

"I'll definitely make sure he doesn't get a tattoo," I offered.

I joined Danny at his table, and we watched as Angel talked to a guy who was leaning over her amp and chords, each gesturing wildly and nodding in turn. I could feel my anticipation growing, and I turned to Danny and nudged him to see if he was as excited as I was.

I never tired of seeing Angel perform. I've heard her sing and play the same songs a million times but it doesn't matter. When she's on stage, it's magic.

Angel sat behind her keyboard and adjusted her microphone. Then she gestured to the person controlling the lights. A moment later, the stage went dark except for a circle of light around her.

"My first song is dedicated to my best friend, Beth," Angel said into her microphone, to which I gave a loud cheer, "because it's her favorite. It's called *Own Way*."

She cleared her throat and leaned toward the microphone, closing her eyes for a moment. Her fingers fell onto the keyboard, and she began to sing.

*"Well, I don't know how to be your . . . your kind of reverence. I feel so much more in a song than I do a sermon. And I don't think you have the right . . . to tell me what my relationship with God should be like . . ."*

Her eyes were closed, and she leaned into the microphone, her hands pounding the keyboard and her body moving with the beat. The room, which had been filled with chatter and laughter, fell silent, and all eyes turned to the stage. The room was hers.

*"I just need to be me . . . and do my life the way I see it. I don't ask you to follow me. Find your own way . . ."*

I was so engrossed in Angel's performance that I didn't feel someone staring at me until she'd finished the song and was laughingly accepting her applause. My face drained of color when I turned to see whose gaze was weighing so heavily upon me from across the room.

"What's wrong, Beth?" Danny asked, looking at me with concern.

"Nothing."

He turned to see what I was staring at and shook his head. "Do you want me to ask him to leave?"

"No," I said, giving Danny a reassuring smile. "I can handle this."

As Angel began her second song, I approached Charlie, forgetting my anxiety for a moment as I saw who was standing beside him.

"Owen!" I shrieked, jumping into his arms and giving him a hug. He returned it, laughing.

"How are you?" he asked. "Charlie here tells me he keeps running into you."

I shot Charlie a dark look. "Pure coincidence, I'm sure," I muttered. "But how are you? I haven't seen you since . . . I mean—"

"I'm doing good," Owen interrupted, understanding why I couldn't finish my sentence. "I've got a girlfriend. I wanted to bring her, but she was working."

"That's too bad," I said. "But I'm happy for you."

"She sounds really good up there," Charlie interrupted, gesturing to Angel.

"Yeah." I looked at Angel briefly, then turned back to Charlie. "Should I even ask what you're doing here?"

"You did invite me."

"What?"

"You told me about this," he said. "When I saw you at Barnes and Noble."

I laughed at his audacity. "I *told* you about it because you asked. That was nowhere near an invitation."

"You want me to leave?"

"If you're here for anything other than the ambience," I said.

"So, what if I told you I was here for more than that?"

"Charlie." Owen's voice held a warning. I glanced from one to the other, realizing more was going on than I was being let in on.

"Okay, we need to settle this," I said, grabbing Charlie's arm and leading him to a far table. "I can't have you popping up everywhere like this. What do I need to say to get you to leave me alone? Rumpelstiltskin?"

He laughed and looked down at his hands.

"Seriously, Charlie," I said.

"I want another chance, Beth."

"You can't have one," I exclaimed. "I'm married. I belong to someone else now."

"No," he said, his expression mirroring the pain in his voice. "You can't. You're mine; you've always been mine."

"Come on, Charlie!" I could feel a lump in my throat. "Stop it. Mike is a good man; I know *he'll* never hurt me."

"Hurt you like I did?"

"You should be happy for me."

"Happy that you married the first guy that came along so you wouldn't have to deal with your feelings for me?"

"That's not fair," I said. "You don't know anything about our relationship."

"I know he doesn't challenge you." Charlie leaned forward and grabbed my chin, forcing me to look him in the eye. "I know he doesn't excite you the way I do. Doesn't make you feel the way I do."

"Okay, you've been watching too many soap operas," I said, tilting my chin so it was no longer in his hand.

"He's safe," Charlie insisted. "I know he is. He has to be. There's no way you could have gotten over me that fast."

I looked at him with disdain.

"I didn't get over you that fast," he said.

"You want to know when I got over you?" I asked. "I got over you the moment I read that note from Scarlet. The moment I saw that everything I thought we had was a lie. Yes, a part of me still loves you. Always will—I can't change that. And yes, when I see you, I remember the good times and how it all felt. But even if I wasn't married, even if I said I married Mike to hide from you, even if you said and did all the right things, we would never get back together. You made that choice for me when you cheated. So live with it. Learn from it, and leave me out of it."

"I don't believe you," he said so quietly I had to read his lips.

"Argh!" I let out a frustrated growl. "You are *such* a guy."

I stood and walked off, reclaiming my seat next to Danny and refocusing on Angel, who was now into her fourth song. I decided that Charlie was like a rabid dog or a bear. If I held perfectly still and didn't look him in the eye, he'd go away. And if he touched me, I'd roll into the fetal position and try not to whimper.

# Chapter 21

*And the king said unto them, I have dreamed a dream, and my spirit was troubled to know the dream.*

—Daniel 2:3

"I had the craziest dream the night of Angel's show. I mean, I have crazy dreams all the time, but for some reason, this one stuck in my head, you know? It's like I couldn't stop thinking about it. Does that mean it's important? I mean, should I tell you about it?"

"If you think the dream is worth sharing," Dr. Farb says.

"It was so trippy. Mike and I were married, but we lived in an RV. We were driving and driving, and I was getting carsick.

"'Will you pull over at the next rest stop?' I asked him.

"The sun was shining down so hard I could feel it burning my skin as I ran to the rest stop bathroom. I couldn't see my reflection in the mirror and there was no soap in the dispenser. When I came out, it was dark, the only light coming from the neon diner sign. I looked around but couldn't see Mike or the RV. My heart began to pound. I ran into the diner.

"'Do you have a phone?' I asked the lady behind the counter. She pointed and went back to wiping the counter, as if panicked *women were a regular part of her day.*

"I ran to the phone and dialed Mike's number.

"'Hello?'

"'Mike, where are you? Why did you leave without me?' I cried into the phone.

"'Who is this?'

"'What? It's me! Beth!'

"'Who? I think you have the wrong number,' Mike said.

"I could hear a woman's voice in the background so I hung up. I looked around the diner and saw Charlie. I was so relieved, I ran over to talk to him. To see if he could give me a ride. To see if he would take me back. When I got to the table, he was sitting with Scarlet. I knew it was Scarlet, even though she looked like Angel. Neither of them knew who I was. I threw a plate at the wall, but when it broke, it slid to the floor like water instead of ceramic.

"I ran outside, and Stan was standing by an old, broken-down car. He was waving me over.

"'I can give you a ride,' he called. I didn't know how because the car was clearly not working.

"'I have a present for you,' he told me. When I walked over, he reached into the back of the car and pulled out something wrapped in a purple shirt. I opened it, and it was a baby.

"'Why are you giving me a baby?' I asked.

"'Because I don't want it,' he said."

I woke up in a cold sweat, the sheets beneath me damp and sticky. I lay there, staring at the ceiling until my heart slowed down and my head stopped spinning. I pulled myself out of bed and got into the shower, sitting under the stream of water until it began to run cold. Then I stood in front of the bathroom mirror, huddled in the small bit of warmth my towel provided. I could barely see my reflection because the mirror was covered in steam. I stared at my foggy reflection and remembered the dream.

The steam began to evaporate, and my blurry image began

to clear. I don't know how long I stared at it, but a loud knocking startled me back into the moment, and I realized that my hair was almost dry and the bathroom had grown cold.

"Beth?" Lady's voice called through the front door. "Are you home? I can see your car out front. Beth! You're not answering your phone, and I've been trying to call you all day. Beth!"

I trudged over to the door, still half in stupor. I opened it and said hello. Then I left her in the entryway while I went into my bedroom to put some clothes on.

"Are you feeling okay?" Lady asked, shutting the door and following me into my room. "You don't look so good."

"Had a bad dream," I mumbled, throwing a sweater over my head and pulling on the jeans I'd worn the day before.

"Mike still fishing?"

"Yeah," I said, pulling my hair into a ponytail. "He'll be back tomorrow night."

"Great!" Lady clapped her hands. "Then we can celebrate."

I turned to her and frowned. "Celebrate what?"

"I'm engaged," she squealed, holding out her hand to display the tiniest ring I'd ever seen.

"Chance proposed?" I asked in shock.

"Kind of." She pulled her hand back and stared lovingly at the ring. "I gave him my version of Mom's ultimatum."

"Which was?"

"He marries me or moves out."

"That's truly romantic."

"He said he was planning on asking me anyway," she said. "I just pushed up his timetable a little."

"Wait a minute." I shook my head in confusion. "Last time I talked to you, Chance had been AWOL all night."

"Oh, yeah." Lady giggled. "He explained all that. I guess the party he was at turned into a big make-out session, so he and some friends went over to another guy's house to play video games, and he just fell asleep."

"It's that easy?" I asked. "You weren't mad at him for not calling to tell you what was going on or anything?"

"We are both still getting used to living with people," Lady explained as if I were missing something that should have been obvious. "He'd never had to call me in that situation before."

"So, when's the happy day?" I asked, falling back on the couch.

"Yeah." Lady paused. "We for sure want to wait until after I have the baby. I mean, we're thinking in, like, a year or so."

I couldn't help laughing. "Isn't that exactly the same time-table you had before? Two years after you move in you'll get married? Nothing's changed, except that now you have a new piece of jewelry."

"Why are you being so negative?" Lady asked, her hands on her hips. "I thought you'd be happy for me. Isn't this what you wanted?"

"I am; it is," I said. "I want to be . . . but—"

"But what?" She stopped and looked closer at me. "What's going on with you, Beth? Are you just transferring your issues onto me?"

"What is that supposed to mean?"

"You're just trying to ruin it for me because you're so unhappy."

"I'm not unhappy," I muttered. "And you're not exactly the model of good judgment over there, so—"

"Are you serious?" Her voice rose to a shriek. "At least *I'm* not afraid to live my life. At least I'm not afraid to make a mistake or two. You're so terrified of doing anything wrong you've mapped out your entire life according to all the sitcoms we used to watch."

"That doesn't even make any sense. I—"

"You're faking it." She pointed her finger in my face. "You're faking it, and you think that my marriage to Chance is just as fake. That's why you're upset."

"At least I didn't get knocked up," I said before I could stop myself.

Lady held up her hands and took a few steps back. "I thought you, of all people, would be happy for me, but if this is the kind of congratulations I'm gonna get from you . . ."

"You're making a lot of accusations, but I'm still the first person you call when you need something," I said. She was already at the door.

"You need to figure out what you want," Lady yelled over her shoulder, "before you start telling other people what they should want."

She was in her car and driving off before I could stop her. I walked back into my apartment and collapsed on the couch, staring at the ceiling and wishing Mike were back from fishing so I could wail about the injustice of being so brilliant and insightful when no one listens to me.

# Chapter 22

*We are responsible for the home we build. We must build wisely, for eternity is not a short voyage.*

—Thomas S. Monson, "Hallmarks of a Happy Home," *Ensign*, November 1988, 69

"*Where do you think you fit in with your family?*" *Dr. Farb asks, clasping his hands in front of him and crossing one leg over the other.*

"*Oh, that's easy. Let's see, Jeri's the creative one,*" *I tick off a finger for each sister.* "*Rory is the overachiever, Lady's the black sheep, and I'm the funny one.*"

"*So, you see everyone's roles as clearly defined.*" *Dr. Farb looks at me over the tops of his glasses.*

"*Obviously we're not just those things, but . . . well, you're the one that asked the question.*"

"*We've discussed before your inability to be serious,*" *Dr. Farb says.* "*Do you feel like you hide your real feelings behind your jokes?*"

"*It's not that.*" *I become defensive.* "*I've told you already that I was picked on a lot when I was a kid. I learned that if I could make everyone laugh, then they would like me. That's how I made friends.*"

It didn't matter that I was awkward or poor. That's the power of humor."

Dr. Farb watches me, clasping and unclasping his hands.

"I get it, Dr. Farb. I know what you're trying to say. You think that humor is my way of denying the rejection I suffered in my childhood and boo-hoo-hoo, all I really need is a good cry, right? But I think a good cry is overrated because guess what? I've tried it."

"So you don't let yourself cry?"

"What? What is this?" I shriek and jump to my feet, pointing at Dr. Farb accusingly. "So what if you've read a couple of books and taken a couple of tests? You don't know me. You're here because I'm paying you to be here. And when my hour is up, you'll go on with your life and forget all about my problems, but I'll forever repeat to myself what we've talked about in here. That's what therapy is. Your own family gets sick of hearing about your problems, so you pay someone else to do it."

"You're very angry right now, Bethany," Dr. Farb says. "You seem resentful of the idea of therapy, and yet here you are. Why do you think that is?"

"I don't know." I sink back into my chair. "Because I'm tired of doing the same stupid thing over and over. I'm tired of hurting the people I love and letting them hurt me."

"So what is it about therapy that is really bothering you?"

I sigh, throwing my hands up in resignation.

"The fact that I'm paying someone to care about me. The fact that you'll always mean more to me than I mean to you."

Dr. Farb picks up his notebook and makes a note. "Very good, Bethany. I think you're finally starting to open up. Now maybe we can talk about what brought you here in the first place."

"You mean Mike?"

"Yes." Dr. Farb nods. "Are you ready to talk about what happened?"

# Chapter 23

I SCANNED MY LIVING room to make sure everyone was having a good time. Or at least faking it properly. It had been a month since my fight with Lady over her engagement, and we'd made up (if pretending like nothing happened could be considered "making up"). To really smooth things over, I'd decided to throw her a baby-shower barbecue, since she was due in a few months anyway.

Thanks to that bright idea, I was now staring at twenty people crammed into my minimalist version of a living room and backyard, trying not to scream "Don't forget a coaster" or "The garbage is over there" every time someone moved.

"How's life in the fast lane?" Angel asked, coming up beside me, holding a can of Sprite and a plateful of chips and salsa.

"Not very fast," I said, reaching for a napkin on the counter beside me—just in case. "Maybe my life is finally slowing down."

"Or maybe it's just the eye of the storm," Angel said, holding her plate up to her face and grabbing a chip with her mouth.

"You're mixing metaphors." I scrunched my nose at her. "Very tacky."

She stuck her tongue out at me and glanced around the room. "Did you invite JoJo?"

"She isn't returning my calls. I haven't spoken to her since that night at Club Sound," I said. "But she sent me an e-mail yesterday with a joke about two fish and an eighties child star."

"The 'like shooting fish in a barrel' one?"

"Yeah. I've already heard it, but it's a start, at least." I clamped my mouth shut as I saw someone slam his paper cup onto a table, a few drops of soda spilling out. "Anyway, what about you? How are the in-laws?"

"Let's just say that I'm having a hard time staging any dramatic monologues." Angel laughed. "After Danny gave his family that letter, they've promised to treat me with more consideration—and they're actually doing it."

"So things are going better with them?"

"I guess," Angel sighed. "At least before I wasn't bored."

I laughed and shook my head. "It would seem that whatever soap opera swallowed us has coughed us up and spit us back out."

"Beautiful analogy," Angel murmured, setting down her plate and pushing it away.

"Hey, Beth," Lady yelled across the room. "Your cell phone is ringing."

"Let it go to voice mail," I yelled back. I turned to Angel and shook my head.

"Oh, I forgot." Angel slapped her forehead. "I was going to ask if you wanted to come to church with me on Sunday. They asked me to teach the lesson in Relief Society and I need moral support."

"Yikes," I said. "You might need more than that."

"Well, the lesson is on—"

"Beth!" Lady yelled across the room again.

"Send it to voice mail," I yelled back.

"No," Lady yelled again. "Someone's here for you."

I sat down my drink and peeked around the corner toward the open back door. There, beside Lady, stood my favorite neighbor, Theresa. I let out a breath and trudged over. I hadn't spoken to her since the first day she'd moved in and had allowed myself to hope that it would stay that way. Perhaps she considered my vintage 1989 Honda a public eyesore and was here to threaten me with city intervention.

"Ah, Theresa," I said with a heavy sigh. "What can I do for you?"

"I'm sorry to interrupt you during your party," she said, peering over my shoulder. "It's just that the mailman delivered some of your mail to us by mistake."

She held up a handful of letters. I took them with a smile and nod, hoping this would be the end of our second encounter.

"So, uh . . ." she peered over my shoulder again, and I turned to follow her gaze, wondering what she was trying to find. "Just having a little barbecue, are you?"

"Yeah." I frowned at Theresa. "My sister is having a baby. Was there anything else you needed?"

"Daniel!" Theresa suddenly screeched, making me jump about a foot in the air. "I thought I saw you walking in."

Danny smiled and waved as Theresa pushed past me and rushed up to him.

"How are you, young man?" she asked, patting his arm. "I haven't seen you since Will and I moved . . . what was it? Five years ago?"

"Mrs. Horrison." Danny smiled. "How are you? I know my mom's been missing that nut bread you're so famous for."

"Oh, you devil." She laughed. "How is your mother these days?"

I watched the scene unfold in shock. Though she wasn't being nice to me directly, she was in my house talking to my friends, and all this without a grimace. Angel walked up and stood beside me, a rueful smile on her face.

"This is that neighbor you were telling me about, isn't it?" Angel asked.

I nodded.

"I guess she and Danny are old friends," Angel said.

"Look at that," I said in awe. "She's smiling and laughing."

Angel chuckled and walked up to Dan, shaking Theresa's hand.

I glanced down at the letters Theresa had handed me and leafed through them. I stopped at the third and last one, curious. It was from the Bennion District Courthouse and was addressed to Mike. I glanced up, my eyes sweeping the room. Mike was joking with Chance on the other side of the room, holding out his hands as if to illustrate the size of something. I glanced back down at the letter and shrugged, ripping it open.

I had to read it a few times before the meaning of the words registered. *Mr. Michael Loxstedt is hereby summoned to the Fourth District Court of Bennion City to answer to the charge of driving while under the influence. . . .* For a moment, I convinced myself it was a mistake, a typo. After all, Bennion City was thirty miles away. But then I remembered Mike's fishing trip and Bennion City's world-famous river, full of salmon . . . and beer cans.

I looked back up at Mike, who smiled at me and nodded before turning back to Chance.

It wasn't hard convincing everyone I was ill, though Angel was predictably more inquisitive, but I put off her questions until she finally gave up and left. Once the last of our friends were gone, Mike wrapped his arms around me and asked if I needed some soup or something. I shoved him away, pushing the letter into his hand and storming off into the bedroom. I slammed the door and leaned against it, my heart pounding and my mind racing. What was I supposed to do? How was I supposed to feel? Was this something normal people got this upset about, or was I weird?

"Baby?" Mike called through the door. I could tell he was leaning on the other side and put my hand up against the wood that separated us, as if to hold him back. "Baby, please open the door. I can explain."

I sighed but remained silent. I wasn't sure if I wanted him to simply explain it away—making me feel foolish but safe, or if I wanted to just be angry.

"Beth?" Mike called again. Something thudded against the other side of the door and I imagined it was his head. Then I imagined it again.

"I don't know what you could possibly say," I called back. "I don't . . . I just don't . . . oh, Mike."

I slid down to the floor and put my head in my hands.

"Beth." Mike's voice was weak. "Look, I'm sorry. You know how hard it was for me to stop drinking. You know what a big part of my life that used to be."

"You're right," I said, my voice dripping with sarcasm. "How could I be so insensitive? Of course you should be allowed to sneak off and drink behind my back. Who am I to be upset about that? Oh, and of course driving under the influence should not be held against you since you probably wouldn't have been in that situation had it not been for your harpy wife."

"That's not what I'm saying," Mike shot back. "Stop putting words in my mouth. I was just saying I had a moment of weakness. It happens to people who are *human*."

"What is that supposed to mean?"

"Look, Beth, I—"

"No," I yelled. "I want to know what you meant by that. Are you saying I don't feel anything? Just because I'm strong; just because I'm not stupid enough to make the same mistakes over and over again . . ."

"That's just it," Mike said. "You expect everyone to be as strong as you. Most of us aren't perfect. Most of us have to fight every day to make the decisions that come so easy to you."

"That's not what this is about," I screeched. "It's about you lying to me. It's about me not trusting you ever again. It's about—like, how could you look me in the face night after night knowing you were lying to me? I mean . . . I just . . . I'm in shock right now."

I sang a nursery song in my head to calm myself down.

"Beth . . ."

*London Bridge is falling down, falling down, falling down . . .*

"Beth—"

*London Bridge is falling down, my fair lady . . .*

"Beth."

"What?"

"Would you please answer your phone?" Mike asked. "It's been ringing nonstop for ten minutes now."

"Oh."

I pulled myself up and opened the door, breezing past Mike as if he wasn't there. I walked over to my phone and flipped it open, frowning. I had ten missed calls and three new messages. I dialed my voice mail and turned my back to Mike.

*"Hey, Beth. This is Joan . . . uh, JoJo's mother. Well, uh— there's been an accident, and we're over here at Jordan Valley Hospital. Thought you might want to stop by and uh . . . okay, I'll see you when you get here. Bye. Oh, we're on the second floor. Bye."*

My heart began to pound, and I pressed the button to listen to the next message.

*"Beth. It's Angel. I just got off the phone with JoJo's mother. I guess JoJo was in a car wreck. I guess it was pretty bad. Dan and I are heading over there right now. Call me as soon as you get this."*

I turned to Mike, my expression frozen in worry. He was watching me quietly.

*"Beth, it's Lady. . . . Uh, Angel's been trying to call you to let you know about JoJo. I don't know if you know, but she's been hurt. We're all meeting at the hospital. She's in ICU."*

I dropped my phone and burst into tears. Mike rushed over and wrapped his arms around me, and I collapsed against him, trying to catch my breath.

"What's wrong, baby?" he asked, rubbing my back gently.

"It's JoJo." My words were muffled against his shoulder. "She's in the hospital."

"What happened?" Mike pulled me back, looking into my eyes.

"They say it was a car wreck," I said. "But I don't believe them."

"What do you mean? How—"

"I think it was Ted."

# Chapter 24

As soon as the elevators opened on the second floor of Jordan Valley Hospital, I saw a cluster of people in front of a doorway down a long corridor. A doctor had just approached them, and I could hear Angel's voice ring out: "But what does that even mean? Can you say that again—in English this time?"

I grabbed Mike's arm and crossed the hall, catching the last few words the doctor said before he turned and walked off.

"Did he just say that JoJo has to stay here for a few more days?" I asked, grabbing Angel's arm and swinging her around.

"Beth? Where'd you come from?" Angel asked.

"What did the doctor say? What happened?" I was impatient.

"Well, uh, what I think—"

"He said she's sustained multiple fractures in her left arm and leg," Danny interrupted. "She's pretty bruised, but she'll be okay. They just want to keep her a few days to make sure there's no internal bleeding."

Mike let out a low breath and shook his head.

"Where's Ted?" I asked in a soft voice.

"He's down in the cafeteria," Angel said. She watched me closely for a moment then rubbed my arm. "He's banged up, too. It was a car crash, Beth. It wasn't anyone's fault."

"How bad?"

"Beth, seriously," Angel said. "You can't really think—"

"How bad?" I interrupted.

"He's got a few scratches on his face and a sprain." Angel crossed her arms, as if I was accusing her of something.

"That's it?" I let out a harsh laugh. "JoJo's all broken up and . . . and—"

"What are you trying to say?"

I turned to see Mr. Warner, JoJo's father, fixing me with a hard look. I hadn't even realized that he, Mrs. Warner, Lady, and Kim, JoJo's little sister, had all turned and were listening to my conversation with Angel.

"I just don't trust him," I said quietly, avoiding eye contact.

"Is there a reason you don't trust him?" Mr. Warner asked. I looked up at him in surprise.

"I'm sorry I said anything." I tried to backtrack. "It was inappropriate."

He waved his hand impatiently. "I don't care about all that. I want to know what you're talking about. Is there something we should know about Ted?"

"Speak of the devil," Angel muttered, nudging me. We turned to see Ted making his way down the hall. He gave a small nod toward us, his expression somber, his stride casual. He had a small cut above his eye, a bruise on his cheek, and a bandage on his right hand.

"Hey guys," Ted said, stopping beside Mr. Warner and slapping him on the back. "Thanks for being here. It really means a lot to me."

"When can we see JoJo?" Angel asked, taking a small step forward so that she was between Ted and me.

"She's stable now," Ted said. "Though the doctors say she

was never in any real danger. I'm gonna sue the pants off the guy who hit us."

"How did it happen?" Lady asked, speaking up for the first time since I'd arrived. I rolled my eyes. No one had even noticed that Ted had completely ignored Angel's question.

"Oh, uh . . ." Ted ran a hand through his hair and exhaled loudly. "Well, we were just driving along and JoJo was telling me to hurry up because she really wanted to get home. So, uh, I stepped on the gas to make it through a yellow light, but this guy waiting to turn left just wasn't looking, and he plowed right into us."

"So, the guy hit you on the driver's side?" I asked.

"What?"

"If he was waiting to turn left," I said, making a motion with my hands. "Then he would have hit you on the driver's side, right?"

"Well, yeah, I guess." Ted glared at me. "I mean, of course."

"Then why aren't you as banged up as JoJo?"

"What?" This time Mr. Warner asked the question.

"If the driver hit them on Ted's side, how come JoJo's the one with all the injuries?" I don't know what I thought this line of questioning would accomplish, but I couldn't keep my mouth shut.

A nurse dressed in tropical-style scrubs approached us, tapping Ted on the shoulder and smiling at him shyly, the generous flesh on her cheeks turning pink. "She's awake now. If you'd like to visit her."

She glanced at the rest of the group with a grimace. "Only four in the room at a time, please."

I glared at the nurse as she trudged away. The bad news with this rule was that I'd have to wait until JoJo's family was done visiting her before I'd be let in. The good news was that I could see her without Ted.

As soon as the Warners and Ted had entered JoJo's room and closed the door behind them, Angel turned on me.

"What was that?" she asked, stomping her foot.

"What was what?" I asked innocently.

"Hey, Mike," Danny cut in. "You want to go get a snack? I think I saw some vending machines around the corner."

"Sure." Mike looked back and forth at Angel and me as he backed away. "That's probably a good idea."

"Can I come, too?" Lady asked. "I'm totally craving nuts right now."

"Look," Angel said as soon as they were out of sight, "I know you think Ted's a jerk. I think he's a jerk too. But of all the inappropriate times to pick a fight—"

"I'm not going to pretend I buy that story of his, if that's what you're thinking," I snapped. "You can't tell me you think that's what really happened."

"It doesn't matter what we think," Angel said, shaking her head. "Starting a fight over it isn't going to help JoJo get better any faster."

"Whatever." I threw my hands up and leaned against the wall, looking away.

"What's wrong, Beth?" Angel asked, her tone softening. "Are you really that upset? They said JoJo's going to be fine, so . . ."

"It's not that," I said. "I mean, it's not *just* that."

"So, then?" Angel prodded me.

"You know how I made everyone leave the barbecue because I wasn't feeling well?"

"Yeah."

"Well, the reason I wasn't feeling well"—I paused, looking down the hall to make sure Mike wasn't within earshot—"the reason I wasn't feeling well was because I found a summons to Mike because he got a DUI."

"What?" Angel gasped.

"I guess it happened on his fishing trip with Jim," I said.

"What did he say?" Angel asked. "I mean, are you sure it wasn't some mistake or something?"

"I'm sure it wasn't a mistake. I think. I don't know—you guys called so we rushed over here. We haven't even really talked about it yet."

"Wow," Angel said, shaking her head. "JoJo married a jerk, you married a closet alcoholic, and I married the son of Janice."

"Gee, when you put it like that."

"I know." Angel nodded, stone-faced. "I've got it the worst. I mean, come on—we're talking about *Janice.*"

"That truly is a rare and wonderful gift," I said.

"What?"

"How you can take anything and make it about you."

"Thank you." Angel gave a small curtsy.

Danny and Mike walked up with a handful of snacks. Lady was a few feet behind them, struggling to rip open a bag of pretzels while holding a soft drink.

"You guys must be hungry," I said, eyeing a Reese's in Mike's hand.

Mike offered it to me with a hopeful smile on his face. I took it without looking at him. I still hadn't decided how mad I was going to be.

"So, how much longer do you think it'll be?" Lady asked through a mouthful of pretzels.

Danny was about to answer, but before he could say anything, the door to JoJo's room opened, and Mrs. Warner, Kim, and Ted filed out.

"Can we—" Angel gestured toward the room, but Mrs. Warner shook her head.

"Jo's talking to Dad alone for a sec," Kim said. She noticed the handful of snacks Mike was holding and nodded toward them. "Do you have anything fruity there?"

I frowned as I watched her approach Mike. She giggled and glanced up at him through lowered eyelashes as she picked a snack from the pile. For a thirteen-year-old girl, Kim seemed awfully interested in a married man.

I felt someone's eyes on my back and turned to see Ted, arms crossed with one shoulder leaning against the wall, glaring at me. I gave him a nervous smile and turned back around. I could hear him walk up behind me and clear his throat. I met Angel's eye

and gave her a scared look. She shrugged, an expression of hopeless concern on her face.

"Beth." Ted's voice was low. "I was wondering if I could talk
to you alone for a moment?"

Mike's head shot up and Danny and Lady turned, not even
bothering to mask their curiosity.

"Me?" I asked stupidly. "Alone?"

"Just for a moment," he repeated, wrapping his hand around
my upper arm. Mike cleared his throat loudly and took a step
toward us.

"Dad!" Kim called, diverting our attention toward JoJo's
door, where Mr. Warner stood.

"Hey, guys," he said with a weak smile. "I guess the rest of
you can go in, now."

"Oh, great," I said with a touch too much enthusiasm.

Ted released my arm and took a step back, giving me a look
that made it clear he wasn't done with me yet. Mike stepped in
between Ted and me, putting his hand on the small of my back
and guiding me toward JoJo's room.

"You guys go ahead," Danny said to Angel and Lady. "You
know the rules. No more than four."

"Oh, come on," Angel chided. "There's no nurse patrolling
the halls right now."

"Angel," Danny scolded. "Rules are rules. Even if there's no
one around enforcing them."

"Of course." Angel rolled her eyes. "Jesus is always watching."

She followed Lady, Mike, and me into the room and closed
the door behind her.

We fell silent as we turned to JoJo's bed. She was watching
us with a small smile that looked almost ghostly against her pale
and bruised face. My heart dropped, and I hung back as Mike,
Angel, and Lady gathered around her. Her left arm was in a cast,
along with her left leg, the toes of which were peeking out from
underneath her blanket. Her left eye was a purply yellow and her
lip was cut and swollen. I squeezed my eyes shut and reopened

them, hoping she wouldn't look as awful this time. When that didn't work, I considered turning down the lights. Or putting a paper bag over her head . . . or mine.

"What's up, gang?" JoJo said in a cracked voice. "Danny getting on your case again, Angel?"

"You know Danny," Angel said. "Rules are his compass, and I am the magnet."

JoJo chuckled then erupted into a fit of coughing. I grabbed a cup of water from the side table and rushed over to her.

"Are you okay?" I asked. "Do you want some water?"

"Don't be so dramatic, Beth," JoJo said, waving the water away. "I'm fine. It's not as bad as it looks. Really."

"So, when you getting out of here?" Lady asked, knocking on JoJo's leg cast. "You've got some major sympathy to milk."

"Yeah, right." JoJo chuckled. "Just a few more days, I guess. No big deal. Just glad it wasn't worse, you know?"

"The car crash?" I asked softly.

JoJo turned to me, and her smile faded. "Yes, the car crash."

I nodded and looked away.

"Won't be long before you're in here," JoJo said, patting Lady's belly.

"I'm counting the days." Lady smirked.

JoJo let out a yawn and squeezed Lady's hand. "Well, guys. I'm pretty tired, so maybe we could pick this up later?"

"Sure, sure," Angel said, leaning over and kissing JoJo's cheek. "Just get better, okay?"

"Yeah." Lady leaned over and gave JoJo an awkward hug. "Take care of yourself."

Mike nodded toward JoJo, unsure of what to do next, so he began backing up toward the door.

"Uh, Beth?" JoJo asked as I was leaning over to give her a hug. "Could you stay for a sec?"

"Sure." I straightened and watched as Angel, Lady, and Mike mumbled a final good-bye and left the room. Neither of us said anything, and I tried not to look directly at JoJo.

"Beth?"

"Uh-huh?"

"Beth, look at me," JoJo prodded. I reluctantly turned to meet her eye, my mouth clamped shut.

"My dad's pretty upset, you know," she said.

"Really?"

"Come on, Beth," JoJo said harshly. "Don't play stupid, now. You weren't afraid to say what you thought earlier, were you? You've got my dad convinced I'm married to a wife-beater."

"Well, aren't you?" I asked, my voice trembling.

JoJo stared at me, taking a deep breath before speaking. "You don't know everything, Beth. You jump to a lot of conclusions, you know."

"Maybe I do," I conceded. "But what am I supposed to think? I mean, things just don't add up and . . . and I have this *feeling*—"

"Are you a detective, then? Or a psychic?" JoJo scoffed. "I mean, I thought we were friends. I thought I could trust you."

"You can trust me," I said, grabbing her hand and clutching it. "You can trust me to do everything I can to protect you, JoJo Mojo."

"That's not your job," JoJo said. "To protect me."

"But I . . . but I thought—"

"Listen," JoJo interrupted. "At first, after the whole thing at Angel's show—I was really mad at you, okay? But then I realized that in your own misguided way you were just trying to help. Ted and I have our problems, I'll admit that. But don't you and Mike? Don't Angel and Danny?"

"I think ours are a little different," I blurted out.

"How?"

"Well, for one, our problems don't put us in the hospital."

JoJo threw up her left arm and looked away. "You're so freaking stubborn. You know that? It doesn't matter what the truth is, does it? You're just going to believe what you want."

"It really was a car crash?"

"Yes!" JoJo exclaimed.

"Okay," I said simply.

"Really?"

"Really." I nodded. "You're right. I have to trust you. If you say it was a car crash, then it was a car crash. I'm sorry."

JoJo blinked at me and then looked down, swallowing hard. "Fine. It wasn't just a car crash."

"What?" I yelped.

"I mean, there *was* a car crash." JoJo stared at her right arm.

"Okay." I paused, searching for the right words. "Do you want to tell me what really happened or . . . do you want me to just trust that you're handling it?"

JoJo glanced up at me. "Am I gonna get an 'I told you so'?"

"Heck, yes, you are," I said. We both laughed, and I grabbed a chair a few feet away and slid it up beside her bed.

"We got into a fight."

"What about?"

"Oh, I don't know." She looked up at the ceiling, scrunching her eyebrows. "I think it started because I was paying more attention to the TV than to him."

"He got mad about that?"

"Just let me tell the story," JoJo said. "Sheesh."

I closed my mouth and nodded.

"Anyway, at some point, he punched me and I fell," JoJo sighed and shrugged. "I got up and told him I was going to my parents' house. That I didn't want to be around him if he was going to act like that."

"But then how—"

"Getting there." JoJo gave me a look. "I ran upstairs and grabbed a few things, and when I came back down, Ted was gone. I thought maybe he'd gone to cool off or something. I mean, I didn't even really think about it."

I frowned, confused.

"So I got in my car and was pulling out into the parking lot." JoJo blinked hard, her face going white. "When out of nowhere, he slammed into me."

I gasped, staring at her in shock.

"It happened so fast," JoJo said. "I don't think the damage

would have been so bad if . . . I mean, I didn't even have time to put on my seat belt."

"That inconceivable so-and-so," I breathed, clenching my fist. "We've got to tell the police. He should go to jail. He's insane; he's a complete psycho, isn't he?"

"Calm down, Beth."

"That's easy for you to say. You've got a morphine drip."

"Beth, seriously," JoJo said, putting her hand on my knee. "I told you all this for a reason."

"I know."

"No. You don't," JoJo said, pulling her hand away and brushing her hair out of her face. "I can tell you're not gonna let this go unless you have the whole story. Ted and I have been seeing a couples therapist for a while and—Ted's really uncomfortable with people knowing this, but he's got a chemical imbalance in his brain."

"Okay," I said. "So, what does that mean?"

"It means that when he's not taking his medicine and he gets angry, he can't control it," JoJo said. "You know how when you get mad, it escalates? You start off kind of pissed, but if whatever is upsetting you keeps upsetting you, you'll get more and more angry?"

"I guess," I said, remembering Mike's DUI.

"Well, for some reason, Ted's brain skips all the middle steps and he goes from like, level-one angry to level-ten." JoJo paused, making sure I was still following her. "Anyway, Ted feels like this problem, and the fact that he has to take medicine for it, means he's weak or something. I didn't realize it until today, but he'd stopped taking the pills again. I don't know for how long, because I can't tell until he gets angry."

I shook my head, my mind reeling. "So, that night? Angel's show?"

"Same thing," JoJo said. "But that was right around the time we found out about his problem, and he was trying out different medications."

"But he's such a jerk," I muttered.

JoJo chuckled. "Medication isn't a personality transplant. Ted has his faults, but so do I."

"Yeah, but . . . but—"

"But what?" JoJo asked. "He's not good enough for me? Who decides that? I don't expect you to understand this, but I love Ted. I want to fight for him; I want to fight for our marriage. It was my decision to lie about what really happened."

I put my head in my hands, closing my eyes and holding back tears.

"Beth." JoJo stroked my hair. "Beth, you fight for the people you love, and that's great. But you've got to stop trying to change everyone, to make everything look the way you think it should."

"So what? I should just give up?" I said through my tears, which were freely falling now. "I should just stop caring? I should just let everything . . . let everything fall apart around me?"

"What are you really scared of?" JoJo asked. "That the people you love will get hurt? You can't stop that. People get hurt all the time, and it's not as scary as you think. It's what makes us stronger."

"Stop it," I burst out, standing and looking down at her. "You think you're stronger? Look at you. You could've been killed tonight. Don't you even care about that little fact?"

"Beth, please—"

"Fine. If you want to get hurt, go ahead. But I'm not that stupid." I walked to the door and swung back around. "I would never let anyone hurt me again."

"Again?" JoJo asked, frowning. "Who are you talking about?"

"What? I'm talking about you and Ted."

"No, you're not," JoJo said. "You said you weren't going to let anyone hurt *you* again. Who hurt you, Beth?"

"Santa Claus," I muttered, swinging open the door and storming out.

# Chapter 25

*A young person's developing concept of God centers on characteristics observed in that child's earthly parents.*

—Jeffrey R. Holland, "The Hands of the Fathers,"
*Ensign,* May 1999, 14

"Santa Claus?" Dr. Farb asks, interrupting me.

"I guess I was trying to be funny."

"Were you?" Dr. Farb pauses, fixing me with a look. "Why is he what came to mind at that moment?"

"What? I'm just telling a story here, and you zero in on one little thing? It was a joke. I already told you that."

Dr. Farb remains silent, waiting for me to continue.

"What?" I ask again. "You want me to tell you about some poignantly traumatizing childhood memory that reveals the reason I made that particular reference at that particular moment?"

"If that's what you want to do," Dr. Farb says, a smile playing at the corner of his mouth.

"Fine." I try hard not to smile back. "I guess the one you want to hear happened when I was three. It was Christmas Eve, and I was lying in bed, wide awake. Mom had said that Santa Claus wouldn't come until I was fast asleep but, hard as I tried, I couldn't do it. I *couldn't drift off. Lady was out cold in the bed next to me, and I remember watching her, wondering how she'd managed it."*

I play with the edge of my shirt, twisting the material in my fingers.

*"I was finally starting to feel my eyelids become heavy when I heard muffled voices. My heart leapt. Maybe Santa Claus was tired of waiting for me and had just let himself in. Maybe he'd brought one of his reindeer with him. I climbed out of bed and tiptoed to the bedroom door, opening it carefully and peeking out. I could see shadows on the living room floor and I distinctly heard Mom say, 'Just put them over there.' This was all the proof I needed. Santa Claus was in my living room. I jumped into the room, a huge smile on my face, prepared to leap into his arms and ask if I could see his sleigh."*

I give Dr. Farb a sad smile.

*"But it wasn't Santa. It was just Mom and Stan, though I knew him only as 'Daddy' then. Mom looked caught, holding a toy pony and a brightly wrapped present, but Stan didn't see me at first. He was leaning over a box, trying unsuccessfully to tape it closed.*

*"'How the heck do you—' he snapped, throwing down the tape and turning to Mom.*

*"'Stan, honey,' she said, pointing to me.*

*"He glanced over his shoulder, finally noticing me. I stood there feeling confused.*

*"'What?' he asked Mom.*

*"'Stan,' she said again, stressing his name and nodding toward me with her head.*

*"'Where's Santa?' I asked, realizing that he definitely wasn't in the room.*

*"'Well,' Mom sat down the pony and the present and walked over to me, kneeling down. 'Santa was running behind, so he asked your dad and me to finish up for him here so he could get everything done in time.'*

*"'Oh,' I said, nodding somberly.*

*"'What kinda garbage are you telling her?' Stan stood up and put his hands on his hips. 'She can't still believe in all that junk, can she?'*

"'She's only three,' Mom said, 'Of course she should still believe in all that junk.'

"I just looked back and forth between them, trying to figure out what they were talking about.

"'I don't want any kid of mine believing in fairy tales,' Stan said, stomping over to us. 'It's embarrassing.'

"He looked down at me and pointed to the presents behind him. 'All of those nice new things are from your mommy and me.'

"I frowned, staring up at him. I already knew Santa asked them to help, so what was he trying to say?

"'Santa's not real,' he said. 'He's a stupid tradition made up by a stupid society that wants to raise stupid kids.'

'Stan!' Mom swung me up into her arms and took a step away from him. She turned to me, touching her forehead to mine. 'Don't you listen to him, Betsy Boo. Don't you listen to him.'

"'Santa's not real.' Stan said it louder this time. 'He's a stupid made-up fairy tale, and if you don't stop believing all that crap, I'm not going to buy you anything for Christmas next year.'

"'Stan, you're drunk,' Mom said, pointing to the door. 'Why don't you just go take a walk?'

"'I'd be glad to,' he said, glaring at Mom and walking to the door. He opened it and took a step out, looking over his shoulder. 'He's not real, Beth. None of it is.'

"I cringed as he slammed the door behind him and did what any reasonable three-year-old would do in the same situation: I started crying."

I didn't say a word to Mike on the drive home from the hospital, and he didn't ask. When we walked in the door, the first thing I saw was the DUI letter sitting on the kitchen counter. I picked it up and stared at it. Mike sat at the kitchen table, waiting for me to speak.

"So, what else are you lying to me about?" I asked, still staring at the letter.

"Nothing, baby. I promise."

I grunted. "Yeah. And if I'd asked you that question yesterday, would your answer have been the same?"

"Listen, Beth." Mike put his head in his hands. "It's not what you think. If you could just let me explain . . ."

"Fine," I said, sighing and plopping down in the chair across from him. "Explain."

"When Jim and I were driving back from the lake, we got pulled over," Mike began.

"Yeah, I deduced that much."

"*And,*" he said the word sternly, "Jim had been drinking. A lot. He told the officer that he'd forgotten his license and then gave them my name."

"How would that even work?" I asked incredulously. "They could have easily looked up the license and seen your picture."

"You'd be surprised," Mike said. "I mean, they looked it up, but they didn't pay attention to the picture. I guess Jim and I look enough alike."

"Wait." I shook my head. "How do I know you're not lying about *this?*"

"Call Jim," Mike challenged. "Ask him. He said he'd take care of everything. He told me I did him a huge favor, and he'd never forget it; that if he'd gotten another DUI on his record, he'd have been sent to jail. What was I supposed to do?"

"I don't know," I said. "I just . . . I don't know . . . wait a minute—the fact that Jim did or did not make you take the fall for his DUI is secondary to whether you drank as well."

Mike stared up at me, his mouth hanging open.

"Well?"

"What?"

"You *did* drink, didn't you?" The voice that came out of my mouth rang in my ears, and it terrified me to realize I sounded just like my mother.

"I took a sip of one of Jim's," he said, refusing to look directly at me.

"And were you planning on ever telling me?"

"I didn't think it would matter," Mike said. "It's not like I was at a bar or anything. It was just me, Jim, and the fish. What's the big deal?"

"The big deal is that you made me a promise that you didn't keep," I said. "The big deal is that you not only *lied* to me, but now you're acting like I shouldn't even be upset about it."

"I'm not saying that. You should be mad, but I'm sorry. What else am I supposed to do?"

"You're not supposed to do it in the first place," I burst out.

I glanced at the clock and cringed, realizing how late it was.

"I'm going to bed," I said. "I've got to work in the morning."

Mike stood, as if to follow me, so I stopped and nodded toward the living room.

"I think you better sleep on the couch tonight." Even as I said it, a stab of pain shot through my body, but I ignored it. "We'll finish this tomorrow."

# Chapter 26

I KNEW IT. I knew he would come visit me today of all days. And there he was, a smug look on his face as he flipped through a book in the Current Affairs section of Barnes and Noble. I held up a finger before he could speak and went off to tell my manager I was taking my lunch. When I wandered back by a few minutes later, he was still there, waiting and looking smug.

"What are you doing here, Charlie?" I asked with barely contained patience.

He held up *The 100 Stupidest People in History,* by Georgette Parks, and waved it at me, his eyes wide with innocence. "Just catching up on my current affairs. Are you working today?"

"Listen, Charlie, you left Charming-town a while ago," I snapped, grabbing the book from him and sticking it back on the shelf. "And the mayor of Stalker-ville's about to give you the key to the city."

"What's wrong, Beth?" he asked, grabbing my hands and pulling me towards him.

"Mike is stopping by to have lunch with me." I pulled my hands out of his and stepped back. "He'll be here any minute."

"Beth." He glanced down at my withdrawn hands, and then looked away. "Listen, Beth. I was thinking about it, and I was thinking maybe we could be friends . . . for real. I know it's possible, we just—"

"What?"

"Don't interrupt," he said with a half smile. "I was thinking you and I . . . and Mike—we could all be friends."

"Are you serious?" I asked, trying not to laugh. "Didn't I already tell you that would never work?"

"I have to have you in my life." Charlie grabbed my hands again. "I don't care how."

"I would love to believe that," I admitted. "But I know you too well. You've been reading eighteenth century poetry again, and now you're trying to live out some epic journey of love with me as the requisite unattainable girl. It's all so very romantic, isn't it?"

"Has it ever occurred to you that maybe you're doing something to encourage me?"

Before I could respond, I heard a familiar voice behind me.

"Is there a problem here, Beth?" Mike asked. I swung around to face him, my cheeks flushing with guilt. Charlie was expressionless.

"Mike, uh, this is Charlie. I told you about him, remember?" I couldn't stop my voice from shaking slightly. "Charlie, this is Mike."

"Nice to meet you, Mike." Charlie extended his hand. "You're a very lucky man."

Mike glanced at the outstretched hand then folded his arms across his chest. "Listen, buddy, I think it's evident that Beth doesn't want you here, so why don't you leave?"

I looked from Mike to Charlie, aghast. "Come on, guys, there's no need—"

"I think I know what Beth wants better than you do," Charlie said, his face darkening.

"Seriously, guys." I placed myself between them, but they ignored me.

"If you know what she wants, how come you couldn't keep her?" Mike took a menacing step toward Charlie.

"Oh my gosh, that is enough!" I put one hand on Charlie's chest and the other on Mike's, pushing them apart.

They both looked down at me, as if just realizing I was there.

"Look, Charlie," I said, turning to him and lowering my arms. "I think you should go."

"We're just talking," Charlie said, looking at me as if I was overreacting. "I'm so glad I finally get to meet your husband and see what all the fuss is about."

"Beth's right." Mike's voice was cold. "You should leave."

"I don't have to leave; this is a public place," Charlie said.

"Charlie," I said in warning.

"If you don't leave," Mike said, taking another step toward Charlie, "I'll certainly make it worth your while to stay."

"And what's that supposed to mean?" Charlie said, letting out a laugh.

"It means you shouldn't be messing around with other people's wives."

"She was mine first."

"Neither of you will have me if you keep this up," I screeched, backing away. It was obvious they didn't hear me as they continued to stare each other down.

"I'm going to ask you one more time," Mike said, his voice barely above a whisper. "Please leave."

"Or what?"

"You know what, *I'm* leaving," I yelled to no one in particular. I turned to walk away but froze at the sound of a loud thud behind me. I swung around just in time to see Mike, who had been shoved against the bookshelf, straighten and catch Charlie's jaw with a left hook. Charlie turned back to Mike, rubbing his jaw and looking possessed. He shoved Mike hard and punched him in the stomach. Mike doubled over and fell against the bookshelf that, to my horror, came crashing down.

"Are you serious?" I gasped, staring at the destruction before me. "You'd think they'd have better support for these things."

By this time, a crowd had gathered around us, and my manager was pushing her way through. When she saw what was happening, she shot me a look of horror.

"Bethany? What's going on?"

"Uh . . ." I glanced down at Charlie and Mike, who were being pulled apart by Jake and another coworker. "That's my husband and that's my ex-boyfriend."

I heard a few people chuckle, but my manager just shook her head. "I think you better take your husband and go home."

"I—"

"Just go, Beth."

I sighed and picked my way through the books strewn across the floor. When I got to Mike, he was standing on his own, holding his gut and looking at me like a puppy who'd just peed on the rug. I glanced over at Charlie, who was staring at his feet with a similar expression. Without a word, I led Mike out of the store.

As soon as we got home, I gave Mike some painkillers and settled him into bed. Then I called Jim and told him Mike was sick and wouldn't be able to come in for the rest of the day. Mike tried repeatedly to apologize for what happened, but I wouldn't let him, deciding I didn't want to hear it until I figured out whether I was flattered or disgusted. I'd never had two guys fight over me before. It wasn't as gratifying as it looked in the movies.

I'd just settled onto the couch when the doorbell rang. I walked over and peered through the peephole, drawing back in surprise. Two men in police uniforms were standing on the other side, one looking thoroughly annoyed, the other staring straight ahead, stone-faced.

I swung open the door and leaned against it.

"Can I help you?" I asked, mimicking what people on TV always do in this situation.

"Hello, ma'am," said the stone-faced one. "Are you Bethany Loxstedt?"

"Yes." I frowned, my heart pounding. I was going to go ahead and assume it wasn't a good sign that they already knew my name. Had Barnes and Noble called the police on us?

"May we come in for a moment?" he asked. "We just have a few quick questions for you. If you don't mind."

"Okay." I opened the door wider and stood back. They walked in and stopped, waiting for me. I shut the door and gestured toward the kitchen table. "Have a seat."

After we sat down, the stone-faced officer pulled out a notepad and clicked open his pen.

"Are you aware that your neighbors, the Horrisons, were robbed last night?" he asked.

"Theresa?" I gasped. "Are you serious? Are they okay? Was anybody hurt? Are you serious?"

The annoyed-looking one chuckled and shook his head. "Mrs. Horrison is under the impression that you had something to do with it."

The stone-faced officer grunted and gave the other officer a dirty look. "That's not what she said, Mrs. Loxstedt. She just thought—"

"Wait, am I under arrest?" I screeched. "How could I? I have an alibi, you know. You haven't even asked me for my alibi yet."

The annoyed-looking officer burst into laughter and tried unsuccessfully to muffle the sound with his hand.

"Why is he laughing?" I asked, hurt. "What did I do? I was just saying—"

"No one is accusing *you,* Mrs. Loxstedt," Stone Face assured me. "What I was trying to say was that Mrs. Horrison told us you had a barbecue the same night it happened, and she was wondering if anyone might have seen anything."

"She implied that there were nefarious characters afoot," Annoyed Face said, nudging Stone Face as if he would think that was funny.

"Okay, guys," I said, my annoyance overpowering my fear. "Why don't one of you tell me what's really going on here?"

"Yeah, Rogers, why don't you?" Stone Face said to Annoyed Face. "Since this is all so amusing to you."

I looked at Rogers imploringly, and he shrugged. "Fine. That crazy lady over there was claiming that you threw a barbecue for the sole purpose of staking out her house—"

"What!"

"And that if we would search the home of each party guest, we would be sure to find her grandmother's pearl brooch," he continued. Stone Face was shaking his head at Rogers in disgust. I just stared at them, wondering if this was some new form of candygram or if they were about to pull out a stereo and begin stripping. I glanced down at Stone Face's belly and decided that last one was unlikely.

"You guys are for real?" I asked.

"Rogers is a rookie," Stone Face assured me. "But if you could give us a list of your party guests, we would like to follow up on that."

"No. No, I don't think so." I leaned back and crossed my arms. "Besides the fact that half of them were either close friends or family, one of them is an old friend of Mrs. Horrison's. Did she mention that? Did she mention that she stopped by here to say hi to him? Or was inviting a friend of hers part of my plan?"

Rogers chuckled, refusing to raise his eyes from his lap.

"Mrs. Loxstedt," Stone Face said in a soothing voice, "I understand that you may feel insulted. But there was a robbery and we have a responsibility to follow up on every lead. Now, whoever did this is still out there, and who knows where they may strike next?"

That last thought sent a shudder through me and I turned to Stone Face. "What happened? I mean, with the robbery? Exactly? I mean, how bad was it?"

"It looks like whoever did it only made off with a jewelry box," Rogers said. "Of course, he had *every* intention of raping Mrs. Horrison, but something must have distracted him—"

"Rogers," Stone Face thundered. "If you don't think every word of this interview is going into my report, you've got another thing coming!"

Rogers's face fell, and he cleared his throat, returning his eyes to his lap.

"Look," I said, suddenly eager to get rid of them. "I did have a barbecue, but it ended early because I wasn't feeling well. About an hour after everyone left, I got a phone call that a close friend was in the hospital. She'd been in a car crash. My husband and I were at the hospital until about 2 A.M., and as soon as we got home, we went to bed. That's all I know."

Stone Face scribbled in his notebook and stood, holding out his hand. "Thank you for your time, Mrs. Loxstedt. Will you be available if we have any more questions?"

"Sure," I said, shaking his hand and then Rogers's.

I walked them to the door and watched their retreating backs for a moment before turning my gaze farther down the street. I could see Theresa's house from where I stood, and as I stared at it, my cheeks grew hot. Maybe I was being paranoid, but I could have sworn I saw her front window curtain move quickly back into place.

# Chapter 27

AFTER THE POLICE OFFICERS left, I checked on Mike to make sure he was still asleep. Then I called Barnes and Noble to see if I still had a job. Since this sort of behavior was unusual for me, told me she'd have to talk to the general manager, but she'd see what she could do. I offered her my firstborn child in thanks, but she said some doughnuts would do. That decided, I hung up and took a deep breath. My next phone call would be harder than the last one, but I knew I had to do it. I'd already decided the night before that I wouldn't be able to work things out with Mike unless I had some questions answered.

"Hey, Mom," I sighed into the phone.

"Hey, honey." She sounded distracted. "Listen, I'm about to walk into a meeting, so do you want me to just—"

"Wait, Mom. I just have a quick question for you . . . do you have any idea how I can get hold of Stan?"

There was a moment of dead air between us, and I cleared my throat to break the silence.

"Stan?" she asked.

"Yeah." I let out a nervous laugh. "You remember him. Married to you briefly. Father of two of your children. Possible drug addiction . . ."

"Why do you need that?" She sounded annoyed.

"Well, uh . . . I just wanted to ask him something. It's dumb, really; I don't even know why I'm bothering."

"Beth," Mom asked again, "why do you want his number?"

"I just wanted to talk to him," I said. "It's been so long and I need to ask him . . ."

My voice faltered but Mom made no sound.

"I need to ask him why he left," I explained. "Or not even that, really. Maybe just ask, like, who he is. I'm trying to understand why I am the way I am, and I figure he's as good a place to start as any."

"Well, I couldn't tell you, anyway. I haven't talked to him in more than ten years," Mom said. "Why don't you ask your stepdad? After all, *he's* the one who really raised you."

"I know, Mom," I sighed. "But it's not the same thing. How do you not understand that?"

"Then I guess you better talk to Lady."

"What? Why would I talk to her?"

"She never told you?" Mom asked with forced ignorance. "Ever since she went to L.A. with that one friend of hers—Cara?"

"Casey."

"Right, Casey," Mom continued. "Well, I guess she tracked him down and paid him a visit. They've kept in touch ever since."

"Oh."

"Honey, I'm sorry, but I've really got to go." Mom's voice was gentle. "Do you want me to call you when I get out?"

"What? No, uh, I'll call you later," I said, already far away. "Thanks, Mom. Bye."

I stared at my phone for a moment, trying to figure out why Lady would have neglected to mention something as important as contacting Stan. Didn't she think I'd be upset when I found out? Was I missing something? Even with these questions, I decided that whatever happened with Lady, it couldn't be worse than almost losing my job or being accused of burglary, so I dialed her number and held my breath.

"Beth? Are you okay?" she asked, answering after the first ring.

"Wow. Did Mom call you already?" I asked, surprised.

"No." She paused. "Why would Mom call me?"

"Why are you asking if I'm okay?" I asked suspiciously.

"Because the last time I saw you, you were rushing out of the hospital after talking to JoJo," Lady said, just as suspicious.

"Oh, right." After everything that had happened today, yesterday's upsets were almost forgotten.

"So, then . . . what's your deal?"

"How come you never told me you saw Stan?" I asked, deciding not to beat around the bush.

"What?"

"Stan? The guy that blew us off when we were kids? The guy we blame all of our emotional issues on?"

"I did visit him," Lady said cautiously.

"Yeah, I already know that much." I sat on my couch and put my head in my hands. "I was asking why you never told me."

"Well, I didn't want you to get mad."

"Get mad?" I asked, confused. "Mad that you saw him or mad that you didn't tell me about it?"

"Both, I guess."

"Lady—"

"What?"

"Spit it out."

"What?"

"Whatever it is that you're trying not to tell me," I demanded. "It's obvious that you're hiding something. I'll bet right now you're tugging at your shirt like you always do when you're hiding something."

There was no answer.

"So?" I prodded.

"I didn't want to hurt your feelings."

"Because?"

"Because, I guess . . . because he blames you."

"Stan?" I asked, shaking my head. "Blames me for what?"

"For the divorce." Lady sounded defeated. "For what happened to him and Mom . . . do you want me to come over?"

"No. I want you to stop avoiding the question and tell me exactly what you're talking about."

Lady let out a loud sigh, and I waited.

"Okay, you realize he's a jerk, right?" she asked. "He's not like us. He doesn't even believe in God."

"Okay."

"Seriously—he's not all there." Lady snorted. "I mean, he thinks that you should have been born a boy. It was okay that I was a girl, but when *you* didn't turn out to be a boy . . ."

"Wait. What?"

"What I am trying to say is that he blamed you for not being a boy," Lady explained. "I mean, he blamed Mom too. But, to him, that was the last straw."

"But he didn't leave until I was four," I pointed out.

"He didn't *leave* until then, but he was already . . . you know, seeing other women."

"So, Stan cheated on Mom because I was born a girl? That's what you're trying to tell me?"

"No. I mean—yes, literally, but that's not what I'm trying to say—he's not all there, right?" Lady's voice quavered. "I mean, when he thinks of you, he thinks of everything that went wrong with him and Mom."

"He told you this?" I asked, shocked.

"Yes and no," Lady said. "I've known some of it forever. I mean, I was six when he left—I remember their fights. And I've talked with Mom about it a little."

"So you were worried about my feelings because Stan really doesn't want me?" I asked. The truth of what she was saying started to sink in.

"No," Lady said and then stopped. "I mean, I know that's what it sounds like . . ."

"He really didn't want me?" I asked again. "He wanted you but he didn't want me? He didn't want me? At all?"

"Beth, this is exactly why I didn't want to say anything."

"He still doesn't want me? He doesn't even want to know what I'm like now? How?" I was swiftly losing coherency. "How can he not? How can a person just not? How could you still talk to him? I don't understand why you get to have him and I don't. I'm the one who does everything I'm supposed to. I'm the one he should want to know. I'm the one . . . maybe if he just talked to me, he'd change his mind. Maybe you misunderstood because I don't—"

"Beth, please." Lady was crying. "I'm so sorry. I'm so sorry I told you. Please just let me come over."

"Don't you dare," I warned. "You're the last person I want to see right now."

I hung up my phone and stared at it. I knew I should be crying. That's what happens next in the movie of life. I cry and wail and get it all out. But even though I kept blinking and swallowing, nothing happened. Maybe I was a fish. Maybe I was too cold to feel anything. For some reason, this thought cheered me.

Then I thought of Mike, still asleep in the other room. Mike. It was his fault. If he hadn't lied to me, I would never have thought to call Stan. I would never have known. I desperately wanted to go back to the time when I didn't know.

I realized then what I had to do, what I should have done from the beginning. It only took me fifteen minutes to quietly pack and leave. The only thing I left for Mike was a note taped to the refrigerator:

*Mike—*

*I'm leaving. I'm sorry, but I know this is for the best.*
*It doesn't matter if I love you. I see that now.*
*Please don't call me.*
*Beth*

# Chapter 28

"Hey, Beth," Angel said, throwing open her door. "I thought you were working today."

"Yeah." I sniffled, switching my duffel bag to my other hand. "Uh, long story. Can I stay here? For a few days?"

"What? Of course; get your butt in here." She stepped aside and took my duffel bag from me. "Is this about the DUI thing?"

"Kinda." I collapsed onto her couch and stared out her front window.

She put my duffel bag in the closet and sat down next to me, looking at me with concern. "So, what happened? What did he say? Did he even try and stop you?"

"Oh, well, he doesn't know yet," I said, glancing at my watch. "I left a note on the fridge, so he should be finding it any minute."

"What?" Angel shook her head. "You left your husband in a note?"

"Did you want me to do it over the phone?" I snapped. "Believe me, this is the simplest way."

"You really think you're getting off that easy?"

"What do you mean?" I frowned.

Angel gave me a funny look. "You really don't think Mike would fight for you?"

I let out a laugh. "I happen to know he'd fight for me. That's part of the problem."

"What?"

"I don't know," I said. "It all happened so fast—I guess I didn't even think about how he'd react to a note."

"What happened fast?" Angel asked. I could tell she was getting frustrated. "You just said you did it in a note."

"Oh, right—you're not psychic."

I filled her in on everything that happened that day, beginning with Charlie's visit and subsequent fight with Mike, followed by my brush with the law and ending with Lady's revelation about Stan. When I finished, we both just sat there.

"Wow," Angel said, breaking the silence.

"Yeah."

"So, then, you left Mike because Charlie's a jerk?"

"No," I said, looking at her like she was an idiot.

"Oh. You left Mike because *Stan's* a jerk?"

"No." I rolled my eyes. "I left Mike because it wasn't going to work, and I finally realized that."

"But you think it's not going to work because of Stan?"

"Would you shut up about Stan?" I stood up and crossed my arms. "This is about self-preservation. The fact that Mike lied to me just shows that you can't trust people, even if you love them. Especially if you love them. And that fight only proves that he thinks I'm a piece of property that he doesn't want stolen."

Angel made a farting sound and looked at me sideways.

"Why are you being like this?" I asked, hurt. "You're supposed to be, like, comforting me or feeding me ice cream or something."

"I'm trying to help you," Angel said. "You are obviously

having some sort of freak-out right now, and I don't want you ruining your marriage over it."

"How often do you and Dan argue?"

"I don't know. A couple times a week, I guess."

"And do you enjoy it?"

"Of course not."

"See?"

"No." Angel gave an exaggerated shake of her head.

I groaned and fell back on the couch. "Because you spend, like, half your week fighting and being miserable and making him miserable."

"Yes, but what do you think we're doing with the other half of the week?" Angel pointed out. "And besides, what's your answer? Just cut yourself off? Avoid meaningful relationships? Only take care of yourself and your immediate needs?"

"It works for the movie stars."

"I give up," Angel sighed. "You've gone mad, and there's nothing I can do about it."

"Nope. It's hopeless."

"Glad that's decided; I've got to go to the store and get some things for dinner. Wanna come?"

"Do you mind if I just take a quick nap?"

"Help yourself." Angel stood and grabbed her purse. "Just don't start rifling through my nightstand."

"Why would I do that?" I asked. "I already know what's in it."

"Ha ha." Angel paused at the door and gave me a searching look. "Are you sure you'll be okay? I'll just be half an hour."

"I'll be fine." I waved my arm. "Now, get out of here so I can get some sleep."

"Take the bed. It's more comfortable than the couch," Angel said.

"When was the last time you washed your sheets?"

"You'll never know," Angel said over her shoulder.

After she left, I sat alone for a moment, the silence hurting my ears. Sighing, I stood and wandered into her bedroom, throwing off my shoes and climbing into the bed. The last thing I thought of before I fell asleep was how, when Mike and I were first dating, he was too afraid to say he loved me, so he'd tap my hand three times instead. It was his way of telling me without having to tell me. The funny thing was, I'd always known what he was trying to say.

Dr. Farb doesn't take his eyes off me, his notebook long forgotten.

"As soon as Mike found the note, he called me, like, thirty times." I admit this with a mixture of pride and guilt.

"And you never answered your phone?" Dr. Farb asks.

"I refused to talk to him." I say this with disgust, as if I was talking about another person's actions. "Angel was furious with me, Lady was furious with me, Mom was furious with me . . . everyone was. But they didn't understand. I knew if I talked to him, I'd break into a million pieces. I just wanted everything to go away. I honestly didn't understand why he was so upset. I thought he would understand that I was just trying to let him off the hook. I mean, Mike's a great catch. He would have found someone ten times better than me in no time."

"But he didn't want to find someone else?" Dr. Farb sets his pen down and watches me closely.

"Yeah." I shake my head and let out a bitter laugh. "And I wasn't prepared for that. I was only thinking about how much I was getting hurt. I thought if I left him, I would save myself the pain of getting dumped a few more years down the line. I never even considered the fact that I was hurting him too. When Angel got back from the store that first day, she told me Mike had called her in a panic, looking for me. She said he was a mess but I didn't believe her. Not because I thought he didn't love me or anything . . . I don't know. I guess I was just being crazy."

"So how long did you ignore Mike?"

"Two days. That's all I could stand. I had no idea leaving him would hurt so much, and I think what made it hurt so much more than I expected was everyone telling me how upset he was. How desperate he was to get me back. On the one hand, it scared me to think that I had that kind of power over someone else, and on the other, it made me start thinking that maybe I was wrong about a few things."

"And that's what made you decide to give him another chance?" Dr. Farb picks up his notebook again.

"That. And some help from an old friend."

# Chapter 29

"BETH, I'M SERIOUS." ANGEL'S face was hard. "If you don't at least talk to him, then you can't stay here anymore."

"If you want me to leave, then just say so." I glared up at her.

"I do want you to leave," Angel said. "I want you to go back to Mike."

"I can't believe this," I said, my cheeks getting hot. "You're supposed to be my best friend, and here you are—meeting with Mike behind my back and attacking me like I was the one who lied or something."

"I just can't believe how unreasonable you're being. If you really want to divorce him, then fine. But I can't believe you won't even tell him to his face. I can't believe you would be that heartless."

I blinked back tears and swallowed the lump in my throat. "You're the one being heartless. You're not even trying to understand what I'm going through or what I'm feeling. I can't do it anymore. I can't give my life to someone who would lie to me. I can't let myself love someone who, at any moment, could just leave and never come back."

"For the last time, we're not talking about Stan," Angel yelled. "Mike is not Stan. If he were, he wouldn't care that you left, now, would he?"

"Mike doesn't care," I assured her. "He's just upset because he feels like he lost a game or something. Because he thinks this will make him look bad."

"What are you even talking about? You know Mike doesn't care about things like that."

"You know," I said, looking at her suspiciously, "if you're so in love with him, why don't you marry him? You seem to think he's so perfect—"

"This isn't about me, so don't even try that." Angel sat on the couch next to me and stared me down. "If you really want to leave Mike, then I will support you in that. But the fact that you won't see him makes me think that you're hiding from something. And you are, aren't you? You're scared because you let someone in and they hurt you—"

"I am not—"

"Let me finish." Angel was stern. "What Mike did, the fishing trip with Jim and all—that wasn't right. I'm not saying you shouldn't be mad about it. But I don't think that's what this is about anymore. What are you feeling right now?"

"I . . . I don't know." I stared at my feet. "It hurts really bad. In my heart, literally, and in my stomach. My mind feels fuzzy and . . . and I don't know, it feels like it did when Stan left."

"Aha," Angel said. "You're trying to get away from Stan and the hurt he caused you. You're running from your feelings for Stan."

"Whatever," I said. "You're not a therapist, so don't try and diagnose me. It hurts because I can finally see that love is an illusion, and humans will hurt each other no matter how much they don't want to. Mike *will* hurt me. If I don't leave now and get away from him, it will only be worse when he eventually does. I mean, if it hurts this much now, imagine how bad it would be if he betrayed me five years down the road."

"So, what then? You're just never going to have a relationship again? You're just going to spend the rest of your life alone?"

"I don't know," I admitted. "But maybe it wouldn't be so bad. I mean, I'm hurting right now, but I also feel . . . safe. I feel like I'm not waiting for the other shoe to drop anymore. It's dropped; this is it. I can't hurt any more than I do right now. What's safer than that?"

"You're being stupid. You know that, don't you?"

"Wow, you suck at this."

"What do you expect? It's been two days and you haven't even talked to him. Ask anybody who's seen him and they'll tell you he's falling apart. He's like a zombie. I just talked to Lady, and she told me when she stopped by to check on him, he just burst into tears and kept asking her what he could do to get you back. That he'd do anything if he just knew what it would take."

"Stop it!" I screamed, putting my hands over my ears. "I don't want to hear that. I don't want to know."

"You need to hear it." Angel stood and leaned over me. "You're being a selfish pig. You're sitting here whining about how you don't want to get hurt and 'Boo-hoo, my daddy never loved me' and 'Look how fragile I am' and you don't even care about what you're doing to Mike. How can I feel sorry for you when you're acting just like the one person who hurt you the most?"

I stared up at Angel in shock.

"That's right, Beth—*you're* Stan."

I stood up and faced her, our noses almost touching. "I never want to speak to you again," I whispered.

I turned and grabbed my purse and stormed out of her house, slamming the door behind me.

❦

I drove aimlessly, listening to angry girl music so loud I was getting dirty looks at stoplights. I hated Angel. I hated Mike. I hated everyone walking along the sidewalk staring at my car as I drove by. Who did she think she was, anyway? Telling me how to live my life? Like she was doing such a fantastic job. And Lady . . . pregnant and unwed. What did she know about love? She was having a hard enough time just getting Chance to stop partying every night. So, what did they know? Why should I listen to them—or anyone else for that matter?

It was dark outside, and I was low on fuel but I had nowhere to go. I glanced at my watch. It was almost midnight. Then it hit me; I knew what I had to do. I had to talk to Charlie. It amazed me that it hadn't occurred to me earlier. After all, it was partly his fault that I'd gotten to this point anyway, what with him popping up everywhere and calling every choice I'd made into question.

I drove to his apartment, my heart pounding harder as each mile brought me closer. I parked out front and looked for his window to see if his light was on. It was. I put my head on the steering wheel and took a few deep breaths. I wasn't sure if I was reacting to the situation itself or if it was because this was the first time I'd been here since our breakup.

I walked up to the door and knocked, wiping my sweaty palms on my pants and switching from one foot to the other impatiently. I was about to turn away, relieved but disappointed, when the door was thrown open.

"Owen?" I asked, surprised.

"Beth?" Owen asked, just as surprised.

"What are you doing here?"

"I live here." He laughed and stepped aside. "Do you want to come in?"

"Oh, yeah. Sorry." I chuckled. "Of course you live here. I'm a little out of it, I guess."

As soon as I stepped through the door, I was hit with all the memories I'd made there. I glanced at the dark kitchen, scattered with dishes and food as usual, and then I looked past Owen into the living room. There was a plant that hadn't been there before, but the faded sofa was the same, as were the Ansel Adams pictures along the walls. I followed him into the living room and sat on the couch, marveling at how it could still feel the same. How a room could feel the same, even if everything else was different.

"What's up, Beth?" he asked, sitting down across from me. "It's kinda late to be dropping by."

"Yeah. Sorry about that." I glanced around the apartment nervously.

"I don't mind." He smiled. "But Charlie's not here. Did he know you were coming?"

"He's not? I mean, no." I smiled, trying to hide my disappointment.

"Is something wrong?"

"What? Why do you ask?"

Owen gave me a funny look. "Because you're here in the middle of the night."

"Is that unusual for me?" I asked, letting out an awkward laugh.

Owen watched me quietly, his expression open and understanding.

"I left Mike," I said. For some reason I was ashamed to tell him this.

"Does Charlie know?"

"Not yet," I said. "That's why I came by. I wanted to talk to him about some things."

"You know, I always felt bad about that whole Scarlet thing," Owen said, his voice soft.

"Why? I mean, don't. It wasn't your fault."

"Well, I knew, and I never told you," Owen said. "And I always felt bad."

"Don't worry about it." I gave him a small smile.

"So, uh, did you leave Mike because of Charlie?" Owen asked.

"No," I said, wondering why Owen looked so uncomfortable. "It was something else . . . Mike lied to me about something."

"Must have been a pretty big lie."

"Yeah."

"Do you want a drink or anything?" Owen asked, half standing.

"Sure." I smiled. "Do you have any soda?"

"Yeah, give me a minute." He left the room and came back a moment later with two Cokes. He handed me one and sat back down, opening his and taking a sip.

I fiddled with mine uncomfortably. "So, do you know when Charlie will be back?"

"No." Owen paused. "He went out for a few hours, so . . ."

"Okay," I sighed. I didn't want to leave yet. I still had nowhere else to go.

"You can stay," Owen offered, "if you want to talk. You know, you were one of my favorites . . . of Charlie's girlfriends."

"I was?" I asked, genuinely flattered.

"Sure." He smiled. "You were never fake with me. A lot of girls put on an act because they want the best friend to like them."

"How do you know I didn't?"

He laughed and looked down at his drink. "I could tell."

I watched him for a moment, and then sighed. "He drank. Mike, I mean. On a fishing trip—and then he hid it from me."

"Oh." Owen nodded.

"It was more than that," I said. "It was a lot of things, but the fact that I had no idea—that I didn't see it coming—that's what really scared me. It was like, what else is he hiding? What else don't I know about?"

"You mean, like another girlfriend?" Owen asked ruefully.

"Ha ha." I gave Owen a dirty look, and then laughed. "Maybe that was part of it. I didn't see it coming with Charlie, either."

Owen cleared his throat and straightened in his chair. "Uh, Beth. There's something I think I should tell you."

My stomach dropped. Owen looked nervous, and that wasn't a good sign.

"Charlie . . . uh, he really loves you, okay?" Owen paused.

"But he's got his issues just like everyone else."

"Okay?"

"And he's doing the best he can, trying to figure out who he is and what he wants out of life and—"

"Owen?"

"Yeah?"

"Get to the point, please."

"He's still seeing Scarlet."

"I'm sorry?"

"He's still dating her. In fact, he's with her right now."

I don't know why, but I began to laugh. I laughed so hard tears came, and I was struggling for breath. Owen stared at me, worried.

"Are you serious?" I asked, gasping for breath. "He's hunting me down, telling me he still loves me and wants me back, and he's still . . . he's still—that is the most ridiculous thing I've ever heard."

"You're not mad?"

"Maybe I should be," I said, shaking my head and leaning back. "But honestly, I'm relieved. And, come on, how is that not funny?"

"I don't think it's funny." Owen was looking at me as if I were having a breakdown.

"It's not nice," I admitted. "But I would have deserved it if I'd left Mike for him. Wow. He's with her right now. Does she know about me?"

"A little, but not everything," Owen said. "I think Charlie kind of uses you to make her insecure."

"That's not cool." I frowned, feeling sympathy for her for the first time.

"There's things you have to know about Charlie, though. To understand him," Owen said, running a hand through his hair. "He didn't have the best childhood."

"You mean, because his mom died?" I asked.

"It was more than that." Owen looked at me, debating how much he should reveal. "His dad was kind of cold. That's just how he was; and when Charlie would cry or show emotion, he'd get in trouble. I think feelings really threatened his dad. So Charlie hid in books."

"Yeah, I can see that," I said. One of the things that brought Charlie and me together was our love of literature.

"In some ways, books became more real to him than his family," Owen continued. "He learned about how the world worked from Poe and Salinger."

"And that's why he's a two-timing jerk?"

Owen chuckled. "I'm not trying to make excuses for him, okay? It's like he's trying to live out his own epic novel, but he's set himself up so that he'll never be happy because of it."

"What do you mean?"

"He's already decided how his life should look." Owen leaned forward, gesturing with his hands. "When it stops looking like he thinks it should, he does things, dramatic things, to get it back on track. Like with you and Scarlet—he met her at a play and was attracted to her. To him, that meant they were *meant* to be together, but when he saw you again afterwards, he still wanted to keep you."

"Okay." I frowned, trying to see where Owen was going with this.

"He wasn't thinking about how you'd feel when you found out or how he'd choose between you two. He was thinking about fate and feelings and this epic journey he was on. He doesn't think what he did was wrong because it was fate that did it, not him."

"Then why did he try to get me back? It seems like fate made that choice for him when I married Mike."

"That's where things get messy, because life isn't about fate or superficial feelings. He really does love you, and according to his idea of the world, that means he should still fight for you. But he also loves Scarlet, so he's waiting for fate to tell him which one he loves more."

"That's completely retarded."

"Not to him," Owen pointed out. "To him, the fact that he's

acting out of love means that his actions are pure."

I stared at Owen, an idea beginning to settle into my brain but not presenting itself yet.

"Charlie's a great guy," Owen said.

"I know," I said, distracted. "I know he is."

"Do you?" Owen asked. "Because I know it's hard to see. If he could just grow up a little. Just realize that life isn't a fairy tale. Life is hard, and love is harder. He spends all his time fighting for these feelings, these grand passions, but he should be fighting for what's real. What you guys had was real; what he had when he met Scarlet wasn't. Now it's kind of reversed itself."

"How so?"

"Well, Scarlet loves him. She's good for him, I think, but now he's running after you even though he can't have you. Especially because he can't have you."

"So what's it going to take, then?" I asked.

"What?"

"What's it going to take," I repeated. "For him to realize what's real, what's worth fighting for and what's not?"

"Losing it, I guess."

"I have to go," I said, standing up so fast I knocked my drink over. "Sorry. Oh, sorry."

I dropped down and picked up the drink, trying to stop the soda from spreading.

"Don't worry about it." Owen stood and took my drink from me. "I'll take care of it. This is a bachelor pad, right?"

"Yeah." I gave him a grateful smile. "Thanks, Owen."

"Hey, I owe you one."

I hugged him tightly, sniffling. I pulled back. "You're a great guy, too. You know that?"

"Get out of here." He laughed, waving toward the door.

I ran out to my car and jumped in. It was pitch-black outside and I was grateful that the roads were deserted as I sped down them. Owen had helped me realize what I needed to do. I was going home, and nothing could stop me.

# Chapter 30

Okay, maybe one thing could stop me.

When I pulled up to my place, I saw Angel's car in my parking spot. I frowned, looking at my watch. It was almost 2 A.M., and as much as I tried, I could not think of one good reason why she should be there. Then I remembered our conversation earlier and how sympathetic she'd been about Mike. Maybe she'd come by to comfort him and they'd lost control of themselves. Maybe they were wrapped in each other's arms, wondering why they hadn't realized their love for each other sooner. Maybe they were laughing at how naive I was to think that I could just come and get Mike back any time I felt like it.

I pulled out my cell phone and dialed Danny's number, hoping he would assure me that he was with Angel and Mike, and they were at that moment gathered around a picture of me, marveling at what a precious jewel I was.

"Hey, Beth," Danny said, his voice groggy. "What's wrong?"

"Hey, where are you?" I asked. "Where's Angel?"

"What do you mean?" Danny began to sound more alert. "I thought Angel was with you."

"Oh." My heart sank. "Thanks, Danny. Sorry I woke you; go back to sleep."

I sat in my car, staring at the lit window of my bedroom, trying not to scream. I decided to try the one thing that I hadn't tried through this whole mess. I folded my arms, bowed my head, and prayed.

Now, let me just say that I am not a praying person. I love the Lord, and I believe in my religion and all that, but I'm a logical person primarily, and it always seemed to me that prayers were more for saying "what's up?" and "thank you." Everything else a person should handle on her own. But it occurred to me that I wasn't handling this situation very well, and perhaps a little otherworldly guidance would at least give me the strength to face the betrayal before me.

*Dear Heavenly Father.* I paused, trying to pretend I didn't feel stupid praying in my car in the middle of night. *Uh, thank you for all my blessings . . .*

I shook my head and laughed. This wasn't working, so I got out of my car and looked around. There was no one in sight, so I knelt by a large tree in my landlord's front yard and took a deep breath.

*Okay, God, here's the thing. It's not like I think I deserve your help; in fact I'm pretty sure I don't. But I figure if it's true what they say—about how you love each of us like children and count all our tears and things like that—then maybe you'll help me anyway. I know I'm pretty selfish; I didn't used to think so because I spent so much time trying to help people and telling them what to do. But after this whole thing, I don't know. Or I could say it's not my fault. That if Stan had been the perfect father or if Charlie hadn't cheated on me . . . but none of that matters. It's my fault if I turn into Stan and start running away from my problems; it's my fault if I turn into Charlie and hide behind my intentions. I guess what I'm trying to say is that Mike is really great. I mean, he's pretty much perfect. For*

*me. And he's nice to me and he loves me, and I really don't want to
lose him anymore. So, if there's a way that maybe I could keep him,
even if for just a little longer, I promise I'll earn it. Thank you. Oh,
and I say these things in the name of Jesus Christ. Amen.*

I stood and brushed the grass off my pants, and then looked
back over at Angel's car, just to make sure it was really hers. I was
feeling better after my prayer, but I still couldn't shake the image
of her and Mike locked in a passionate embrace. I paused at the
door, trying to hear. The sound of Angel's laughter floated out to
me, and I could feel tears in my eyes. I flicked one away and put
my hand on the door.

When I threw it open, both Angel and Mike turned to me
in shock and I stared back, equally shocked. Mike was sitting at
our Casio keyboard and Angel was standing a few feet behind
him—a pen in her mouth and a piece of paper in each hand.

"Why aren't you guys naked?" I finally asked, breaking the
silence.

"You're back," Mike said, standing. The look on his face
broke my heart all over again.

"What do you mean, why aren't we naked?" Angel asked, the
pen still in her mouth.

"I saw your car outside," I said, pointing behind me. "And
when I called Danny, he thought you were with me."

Angel took the pen out of her mouth and stuck it behind her
ear. "That's because after our fight, I went looking for you."

"Oh." I glanced back at Mike, who was looking at me like if
he blinked I'd disappear.

"I came up here because I didn't know where else to look for
you," Angel continued. "And I ended up talking to Mike about
what he could do to get you back."

"Oh," I said again. Angel gave me a look that said, "Don't
you feel stupid?" And I did.

"So, why are *you* here?" Mike asked quietly.

"I came back," I said. "Because I . . . I want to come back."

I looked at Angel and then the keyboard and I frowned. "So,
what were you guys doing, then?"

"Mike is writing a song for you," Angel said, waving toward the keyboard proudly. "And I am helping. That is my specialty, after all."

"You wrote me a song?" I asked Mike, clutching my hand to my heart.

"Baby." Mike paused and shoved his hands in his pockets. "Don't you know I'd do anything?"

"Oh, Mike." I rushed forward and wrapped my arms around him. He held me so tight I could barely breathe, and I buried my face in his shoulder, my tears soaking through his shirt.

"That's my cue to leave," Angel said, slipping out without us noticing.

We stood like that forever, neither of us wanting to pull away. I finally leaned back so that I could see his face.

"Mike, I'm so sorry."

"No, Beth, I'm sorry," he said. "I'll never lie to you again. I'll never drink again. I'll never go fishing again; I'll never leave the house again—"

"Shut up," I laughed. "Now you're just being unreasonable."

He brushed a strand of hair out of my eye and swallowed. "I don't know what I would have done."

"Stop it," I said. "I'm back; I'm done being stupid for a while."

"Promise?"

"Promise." I leaned against him and sighed. "I don't know what's wrong with me, baby. I don't know . . ."

"Don't worry," he murmured. "We'll figure it out."

"Hey, don't you have a song for me?" I asked.

"Oh." Mike's cheeks turned red. "It's not finished yet."

"I don't care." I walked over to the keyboard and ran my hand along the keys. "Play me what you have."

"It's just the first verse and the chorus." Mike sat down at the keyboard. "And it's kind of cheesy."

"Well, cheese is my middle name." I put my hands on his shoulders and nuzzled his neck.

"Wow, what happened?" Mike asked.

"What do you mean?"

"You wouldn't even take my phone calls a few hours ago." Mike looked up at me. "Don't get me wrong—I'm happy you're back. But what made you change your mind?"

"I realized that if you want to screw up your life by making the conscious choice to put up with me, then you deserve what you get," I said. "And I'll probably get hurt again. But the moments in between—the time I get with you—is worth it. So, do your worst; I'm ready."

Mike chuckled. "You need therapy, you know that?"

"Yes, I do." I smiled. "Now play my song."

It was awkward and halting, and Mike kept pausing to remember what keys to play, but I loved it.

*We spoke briefly just the other day*
*And I forgot to say what you meant to me*
*But sometimes words just get in the way . . .*
*But still, how have you been?*
*I'm falling asleep to the thought of you*
*These words sound cheap to what I wanted them to*
*And I can't seem to get through to you*
*Through to you . . .*

# Chapter 31

*When Jesus understood it, he said unto them, Why trouble ye the woman? For she hath wrought a good work upon me.*

—Matthew 26:10

"I was thinking about the whole Adam and Eve thing again." I beam at Dr. Farb across from me. "About how if they couldn't get it right, how could anyone else? Well, I don't know, but . . . I don't think that's the point. It's not about doing it right, or 'perfect,' it's about just doing it. You know? Deciding something's worth fighting for and fighting for it."

Dr. Farb sets his notebook down and smiles. "I couldn't have said it better myself."

# Epilogue

"HAPPY ANNIVERSARY!" ANGEL CRIED as soon as I answered the door.

Mike and I had decided to throw a small party to celebrate our first anniversary, since so many of the people invited were directly involved in helping us get to this point. At that moment, my little sisters were in the backyard, trying to attract the attention of a few boys who were playing basketball next door, while Mom and Lady were having a friendly argument over the pros and cons of using an epidural. Chance and my stepdad were deep in conversation about gardening, a surprise mutual interest that Lady was a little too delighted about them discovering. I'd invited JoJo and Ted, but they were at a couples retreat and had promised to take Mike and me to dinner when they got back.

"Thanks." I smiled, stepping aside so she could walk past. "Just set the present on the table, and there's food over there. Where's Danny?"

I followed her into the kitchen and grabbed a carrot to munch on from the salad tray.

"He got stopped outside by your favorite neighbor." Angel rolled her eyes. "Even after she practically accuses you of robbing her, he's still the perfect gentleman, as always."

"Did I ever tell you? They found out who did it."

"Really?" Angel's eyes lit up.

"It was the babysitter in the closet with a candlestick," I said.

"What?"

"I guess the night she'd stopped by here, she went out to a play or something, and the girl they had babysitting their kids invited her boyfriend over," I explained. "And he wandered off at some point, but the girl didn't think anything of it. Then she finds out Theresa was robbed right before he gets a new stereo installed in his car. I guess she tried to keep his secret but eventually felt so guilty she went to the cops."

"Wow."

"That's not the best part." I laughed. "The boyfriend lives down the street, and his parents are good friends of Theresa's. Or were."

"Hey, baby, what's going on?" Mike came up behind me, wrapping an arm around my waist and nodding a greeting at Angel.

"Just gossiping." I smiled up at him, kissing his cheek.

"Ugh." Angel made a gagging noise. "You guys are like newlyweds all over again. Maybe *I* should sign up for therapy."

Chance called Mike over to settle a debate about springtime planting.

I turned to Angel. "Listen, hon. I've got some kind of bad news."

She visibly braced herself.

"I invited Chandra Higgs."

She relaxed then scrunched her face into a fake pout.

"But why? We haven't seen her since JoJo's wedding."

"I couldn't help it," I said. "She called me, all excited because she's engaged and wanted us to hang out so I could meet him. I just figured inviting her to this would mean that at least I'd get a free gift out of hanging out with her, right?"

Angel shrugged and glanced around the room, her eyes settling on Lady. "Wow, she's huge. When's she due?"

"Two weeks, now," I said. "I know. It's crazy to think she's actually going to have a baby. It's like we're real grown-ups."

"I wouldn't go that far."

Danny walked up and smiled at me expectantly. I looked back at him, confused, so he turned to Angel.

"Did you tell her yet?" he asked.

"Tell me what?"

"Thanks for ruining my big moment, Danny." Angel scowled at him and then turned back to me. "I didn't want to crowd the party with stuff about me but—"

"What?"

"I just got a call from an agency in L.A. that I sent my demo CD to, and they want me to come out and audition." Angel squealed so loudly the whole room stopped talking and looked at her.

"Wow, Angel! That's amazing," I said. I was excited for her, but I couldn't help feeling a pang of worry that I would soon be left behind.

"And?" A voice said behind me, and I turned in surprise to see that Mike was looking at Angel as if she should say more.

"And you're coming." She grabbed my hand and squeezed it.

"I am?" I frowned. "Why? I mean, that would be awesome . . . but why?"

"Because," Mike said, grabbing my shoulders and turning me around, "I think it's time we saw Stan."

"What?"

"I think the only reason he never wanted you," Mike said, "is because he never knew you."

"But, Mike." I gave him a small smile. "I just got *out* of therapy; do you really want to send me back?"

He laughed and hugged me. "It can't be that bad. And I'll be there with you the whole time."

"And Danny and I will be with you when we're not too busy with my fancy new agent," Angel added.

"I don't know what to say." I looked from Angel to Danny to Mike. "Except that I'm a little freaked out you guys are planning stuff behind my back."

Angel opened her mouth to respond but was stopped by a wail of pain from across the room. Lady was falling to the ground, clutching her stomach while Mom valiantly tried to hold her up. We all rushed forward at once while Lady kept screaming, "It's coming, it's coming! Help!"

Mom took control of the situation, handing Lady to Mike and Dad while she commanded Chance to pull the car up and me to find Rory and Jeri. While we all rushed about, trying not to dissolve into a complete state of panic, Danny stood by awkwardly. His only opportunity to help came with a knock at the door, which he rushed to answer. He was inviting Chandra and her fiancé in as we were all trying to squeeze past. Chance was outside, honking the horn, while Rory and Jeri kept screaming, "Is Lady okay? Why is she crying?" Mom was trying to direct Mike and Dad, who were now carrying Lady, through the door, with Angel and me following behind, calling out words of encouragement to anyone who might need them.

I noticed Chandra on my way out and paused.

"Hi, Beth," she said, glancing around her in confusion. "I'm sorry we're late."

"Don't worry," I said, breathless. I smiled at the man standing beside her: A tall, beefy Tongan with a toothy grin. "Is this your fiancé?"

"Oh, yes." She gestured to him with a proud smile. "This is Liahona."

"Nice to meet you." I nodded at him. Everyone was piling into the car, and I began to worry that they would drive off without me. "I have to run right now—my sister is going into labor, so do you mind if I just call you when things settle down?"

"Of course." Chandra nodded, then gestured to the present in her hands. "Did you want this, then?"

"Oh, sure." I started backing away, nodding at Danny for him to follow me. "Just leave it on the doorstep. It'll be fine there. Again, I'm so sorry about all this."

I turned to run up to the car, but Chance was already driving off. I stared after it, heartbroken.

"We'll just take my car," Danny said comfortingly. "Look, there's Angel now."

Angel pulled up to the curb and waved frantically at us. I turned back to Chandra and Liahona and shrugged.

"This is some anniversary party," Liahona observed.

"Well, you know what they say about the first year," I called out over my shoulder.

Liahona laughed, but Chandra stared after me, confused.

"Wait," Chandra called out. "What do they say?"

I jumped in the car and turned back to her, smiling. I'd let her figure that one out on her own.

# About the Author

CRYSTAL LIECHTY spent her early years in San Jose, California, but moved to Riverton, Utah, just in time to enjoy her awkward preteens with people she'd never met before.

She is now living in Sandy, Utah, with her husband, Scott, and dog, Vern. They are expecting their first child in December 2006. When not writing or eating cheese sandwiches, she is studying graphic design at Eagle Gate College.

*The First Year* is Crystal's debut novel. For more information on Crystal Liechty and her books, visit www.crystalin-wonderland.com.